LAWRENCE BUSH

Rooftop Secrets

And Other Stories of Anti-Semitism

Commentaries by ALBERT VORSPAN
Illustrated by MARTIN LEMELMAN

Union of American Hebrew Congregations
New York, New York

To Emu, my teacher

Library of Congress Cataloging-in-Publication Data

Bush, Lawrence.
  Rooftop secrets and other stories of anti-Semitism.

  Summary: A collection of eight short stories, each
dealing with a young Jew's confrontation with anti-
Semitism in different periods of Jewish history.
  1. Children's stories, American. [1. Prejudices—
Fiction. 2. Jews—Fiction. 3. Short stories]
I. Vorspan, Albert. II. Lemelman, Martin, ill.
III. Title.
PZ7.B9654Ro 1986   [Fic]   86-1362
ISBN 0-8074-0314-8

Feldman Library

The Feldman Library Fund was created in 1974 through a gift from the Milton and Sally Feldman Foundation. The Feldman Library Fund, which provides for the publication by the UAHC of selected outstanding Jewish books and texts, memorializes Sally Feldman, who in her lifetime devoted herself to Jewish youth and Jewish learning. Herself an orphan and brought up in an orphanage, she dedicated her efforts to helping Jewish young people get the educational opportunities she had not enjoyed.

In loving memory of my beloved wife Sally
"She was my life, and she is gone;
She was my riches, and I am a pauper."

"Many daughters have done valiantly,
but thou excellest them all."

Milton E. Feldman

Acknowledgments

The enthusiasm and creativity of Aron Hirt-Manheimer, my editor, have enabled this book to come to life. The attentiveness and thoughtful work of Albert Vorspan have added depth and substance to the book's content. My wife, Susan Griss, has provided vital, imaginative feedback and affirmation. The generosity of my mother, Jacqueline Bush, has helped me work on this and other literary projects with little interruption. To all, my thanks.

Contents

The excerpt on page xi is from "To Be a Jew," *Breaking Open: New Poems*, Muriel Ruckeyser, New York: Random House, 1973, page 62.

Preface

To be a Jew in the 20th century
Is to be offered a gift. If you refuse,
Wishing to be invisible, you choose
Death of the spirit. . . .
    —Muriel Ruckeyser

What does this proud Jewish poet mean by the "gift" of being Jewish?

Perhaps she's talking about the privilege of belonging to a people that has lasted for thousands of years—the special knowledge that the prayers you say and the holidays you celebrate have been said and celebrated by other Jews for centuries.

Perhaps the Jewish "gift" means our pride in Jewish achievement: the amazing contributions that Jewish women and men have made to the world in science, art, philosophy, medicine, religion, politics, philanthropy, and so many other fields.

Perhaps Muriel Ruckeyser is thinking about the gift of being "different," of being original and unafraid. Sigmund Freud, the founder of modern psychology, said about being Jewish:

> Because I was a Jew I found myself free from many prejudices which restrict others in the use of their intellect; and as a Jew I was prepared to do without agreement with the . . . majority.

Freud felt that his Jewish identity gave him a feeling of freedom and a willingness to take chances—the opportunity to be a pioneer in the world of ideas.

These are some of the deep pleasures involved in belonging to the Jewish people. No doubt you could name other aspects of Jewish identity that you consider to be special. Why, then, would *any* Jew wish "to be invisible," as the poem suggests? Why would any Jew choose "death of the spirit"?

The answer is that for nearly two thousand years the "gift" of being Jewish has been "gift wrapped" in danger and trouble, persecution and discrimination. We have been hurt and harassed for our religious beliefs; we have been herded into ghettos and kicked out of countries; we have been blamed for all the troubles of the societies in which we have lived; we have been murdered. Anti-Jewish prejudice has lasted so long that it has been given its own name: anti-Semitism. That word, and all that it means, is the subject of the stories in this book.

Each story tells of danger and discovery, of fear and faith, of horror and heroism—of a Jewish kid, somewhere in the world during the past five centuries, who decides to claim the "gift" despite its price. For some, this means facing the hatred of enemies; for others, it means facing self-hatred, the anti-Semitism that our hearts absorb from the world around us. For all Jews, the decision whether or not to accept and treasure the "gift" of being Jewish is complicated.

Each tale is preceded by a brief historical introduction and followed with comments by Albert Vorspan, author and a leading figure in the fight for social justice in America. His commentaries will help you think about and discuss different aspects of each story. My hope is that this book will excite you as a reader and leave you with more questions to think about than you had before —for that process of asking questions is the very secret of Muriel Ruckeyser's "gift."

Lawrence Bush

Rooftop Secrets

The Truth about Maria

Today in America, and in many other countries around the world, religion and government are kept separate. Religious leaders do not make laws; government officials do not tell people which religion, if any, to believe in. This principle, called the "separation of church and state," is an important part of modern democracy.

Before modern times, however, most countries were not democratic but were ruled by kings and queens who were not elected. Often only one religion was allowed: Islam in the Arab lands, Christianity in Europe. In Spain, for hundreds of years, these two religions were at war for control of the land.

While the Arabs were in control of Spain, the Jews who lived there were treated fairly. Many great Jewish leaders, such as the Rambam (Maimonides), lived in Spain during this time, which was called the "Golden Age of Spanish Jewry." In the thirteenth century, however, the Catholic Church—the only Christian church at the time—won the war against the Arabs. Life then became much harder for Spanish Jews.

The Catholic Church forced thousands of Jews to become Christians. Those who refused to convert were made to suffer. They had to live in ghettos and wear badges on their clothing to show that they were Jews. They could not ride horses but had to walk everywhere. Most good jobs were closed to them. Often, Jews were killed in riots.

To avoid this persecution, many of the Jews in Spain *did* convert to Christianity. Many of those who converted, however, secretly practiced their Jewish religion. These "secret Jews" were called Marranos, which in old Spanish meant "pigs"—an insulting word to call anyone, but especially a religious Jew for whom the pig is an unclean animal.

The Marranos suffered a great deal. Being a secret Jew was a crime in Spain, and the Inquisition, a kind of police department of the Catholic Church, arrested Marranos and even burned some at the stake. Still the brave Marranos held onto their Judaism in secret for hundreds of years.

Eventually their Judaism became quite different from the Judaism we know today. The secret Jews did not dare to own or even read talmudic books and did not have rabbis to guide them. They had only the Bible and whatever Jewish prayers and traditions they could remember. Because they had to keep their Judaism secret, the Marranos found that mitzvot like resting on the Sabbath or keeping kosher were very hard to perform.

Worst of all, Marrano parents were sometimes afraid to tell their own children that they were Jewish because children, especially young ones, often do not know how to keep a secret. Therefore, until they were thirteen years old, many Marrano children received no Jewish education at all.

This story tells of one Marrano girl who, at the age of eight, begins to realize that she's Jewish. The story takes place in 1492, the year Christopher Columbus sailed from Spain and "discovered" America. (America had already been discovered, of course, by the Indians who lived there.) It was also the year when the king and queen of Spain ordered all Spanish Jews to become Christians or leave the country. It was a terrible year to learn that you were a Jew. As we shall see, however, the discovery of Jewish identity could also bring strength and pride to Marrano children.

Toledo, Spain: 1492

On Saturday morning, Maria da Silva dressed herself for church. Maria was eight and had been confirmed in the Mother of Mercy

Church only the year before. Since then, her parents had twice sent her to make confession to the priest, Father Manuel Alvarez. Today Maria was going to make confession again.

She would enter the dark wooden closet at the side of the church. She would kneel down and speak through the wall to Father Alvarez. She would tell him all the bad things she'd done since her last confession. He would then tell her how to make up for her sins so that Jesus Christ, the Son of God, would forgive her.

Maria thought confession was a little scary and strange—yet it was not really so different, she reminded herself, from her favorite game, hide-and-seek. Her only problem was that she couldn't think of anything really bad that she'd done to confess to Father Alvarez, even after thinking about it all day yesterday!

She had told this to her nurse, Señora Rodriguez, when she came in the morning to wake Maria. "There is always a sin to be found in every heart," Señora Rodriguez told her. "Even the whitest piece of cloth will have its little stains if you look hard enough."

After she dressed, Maria sat on the edge of her bed and thought very hard. She made a list in her head of every time she'd been mad at someone or lazy or had squashed a bug, even by accident. For example, two weeks ago she had pulled a worm out from under a stone in the courtyard and cut it into little pieces. She had done this to feed a sick dove that she and her mother had found at the bottom of a tree. "So is killing the worm a sin or a good deed?" Maria wondered. "Maybe the little birdie died because of my sins? But Momma said it died because it was too sick to eat the worm."

Maria ran downstairs to the dining room for breakfast. She meant to ask her mother about the worm, but Momma, Poppa, and Maria's brother Pedro were nowhere to be found. Often on Saturday mornings it was like this: Maria would be left alone with Señora Rodriguez. When Maria would ask the señora where the family had gone, the nurse always gave the same answer: "They went to give Pedro his training so he can help your father with the bookkeeping." Then Señora Rodriguez would say in a loud voice, "Hurry, now! We have to leave or we'll be late." No matter where they were going—and there always seemed to be someplace to go on Saturday mornings, like it or not—Señora Rodriguez would say the same old thing.

After a while, Maria had stopped asking—but she kept wondering. Wasn't there room in their big house for Pedro to have his bookkeeping lessons at home? If not, why couldn't a servant take Pedro to his lessons in a coach and leave Maria's parents at home with her?

The family da Silva lived in a great stone house in Toledo, a town in the part of Spain known as Castile. Maria's father, Señor Ricardo da Silva, was a tax collector for King Ferdinand of Castile, who had just become the king of all of Spain. Señor da Silva was a rich man, with horses and fine clothing and many servants to take care of his family and property.

Among the servants was the daughter of Señora Rodriguez, Angelina, who worked in the kitchen. She was almost eighteen years old, old enough to be married like Maria's four older sisters, who had children of their own and hardly paid attention to Maria when they visited. But Angelina was not married. She still lived with her mother in the da Silva home, and she *did* pay attention to Maria—attention of the worst kind, the teasing kind.

It happened again this morning. Señora Rodriguez went off to tell the stableman to prepare a horse and carriage to take them to church. As soon as her mother left the dining room, Angelina leaned next to Maria's ear. "I know your secret."

"What secret?" Maria couldn't think of anything she was keeping secret and became very nervous.

"The secret," Angelina said, "for which you're going to burn."

"Who says?" Maria cried. "I will not!"

"Oh, yes, you will. That's what happens to Jews who pretend to be Christians—they get burned at the stake."

"So what?" Maria said. "Maybe it happens to them, but that's because they're Jews. Hurry, now, I'm hungry! I want my breakfast!"

Angelina turned towards the kitchen. "You dirty little Jew," she grumbled. "And to think that *I* have to serve *you!*"

Maria sat with her mouth open. Why was Angelina calling her a Jew? That was the worst thing in the whole world to be! The souls of the Jews, Maria had often heard, would burn in hell forever. The Jews were damned, Father Alvarez said, because they killed Jesus and didn't believe he was the Messiah. And the Jews had horns on their heads!

Maria blew up with anger. "I'm going to tell your mother what you said," she warned as Angelina came out of the kitchen, carrying a plate. "I'm going to tell your mother *and* my mother!" She stuck out her tongue at the servant girl.

"Here!" Angelina said with a scornful laugh, tossing the plate onto the table. "Stick your tongue onto *that* if you're not a filthy Jew."

The only thing on the plate was a stringy piece of meat. "What is it?" Maria said, poking it with her finger.

"It's pork," Angelina said.

"Uch!" Maria made the sign of the cross on her forehead and chest to keep away evil. "You can't eat pork! It'll turn you into a pig!"

"Ha! That's the lie that Jews always tell their children."

"It is not a lie!" Maria said. "My momma said so, lots of times!"

"Then watch this." Angelina picked up the pork and bit off half. "See? I'm not turning into anything."

"That's because you're a pig already!" Maria shouted, running from the table.

Angelina caught her at the door and stuffed the pork into her mouth. "Eat it!" Angelina yelled, shaking the girl by the arm. "Eat it, or else you're a Jew, and you'll burn!" Maria tried to spit it out, but Angelina held her mouth shut. "Eat it, or I'll tell everybody that your whole family's a bunch of Marranos!"

Trembling all over, Maria chewed the pork just enough to swallow it without choking. "Maybe," she hoped, "if I don't taste it, it won't hurt me." At last Angelina let her go, but Maria did not run away. She stood there, waiting to feel her nose growing into a pig's snout; her hands becoming pig's feet; her long, black hair shrinking, disappearing. . . .

They heard the heavy footsteps of Señora Rodriguez on the stairs. Angelina ran into the kitchen. Maria began to weep when she saw her nurse. "What is it, my precious?" the señora said, kneeling at her side.

"Angelina made me eat pork!"

"Oh, the devil take her!" Señora Rodriguez sighed. "My daughter has no heart. She's cruel, and she's nasty—I wish she weren't mine! But come, Maria, come, child. We must go to church. Dry your eyes, now."

Maria was kneeling in the confession box, just as she was supposed to do. She was waiting for Father Alvarez to tell her how to clean away the sin that she had just confessed—the sin of eating pork. Why was Father Alvarez silent? Had she forgotten to say the right prayer? Had she done something wrong?

Finally she heard him clear his throat. "Eating pork," he said, "is not a sin, my daughter. Who told you that it was?"

"My—." Maria was about to say "my mother," but instead she clapped her hand over her mouth. There was something in Father Alvarez's voice, something dangerous, like a snake. She remembered Angelina's crazy words: "Your whole family's a bunch of Marranos!"

"Maybe he doesn't even know it's me in here," Maria thought. The idea took hold of her. Without thinking any more, Maria ran out of the confessional. A line of people, including Señora Rodriguez, were waiting to make confession, too. Everyone seemed to be staring at Maria as she ran out to the street.

Señora Rodriguez caught up with her. Maria moaned and told her nurse that she felt awfully sick. Immediately the señora took the girl home and put her to bed.

Soon Maria's mother, Doña Flora da Silva, came in to see her. "Maria, what is it? Shall we send for the doctor?"

Maria shook her head and turned her face to the wall.

"What's wrong, darling?"

"You lied to me!"

"I did what?" Doña Flora was shocked.

"You lied to me!" Maria cried. "You said if I ate pork I'd turn into a pig—but it's not true!"

"Pork is not good for you," her mother said.

"But it doesn't turn you into anything. That's just a lie you told."

"Well, I told it to make sure that you wouldn't eat pork," her mother explained. "Sometimes you must tell things to a child, even if they're not completely true, so that she won't hurt herself."

Maria began to blubber. "Angelina made me eat it! She said if I didn't eat it, I was a dirty Jew! And then when I told Father Alvarez that I ate pork . . ."

Doña Flora became pale. "Oh, merciful heavens!" she whispered. "Dear God!"

"What's wrong?" Maria said. "What will the pork do to me?"

"Sh, sh, nothing. It's just that . . . pork is an unclean food. But tell me carefully, now, Maria. What did Father Alvarez say?"

"He said it's not a sin to eat pork. Then he asked me who told me that it was. I got scared, Momma, and I ran away."

Maria couldn't talk any more. She just cried and hugged her mother with all her might. "It's all right, my darling," Doña Flora said. "It's all right." But Maria could tell that something was *not* all right because her mother was stiff and cold, with trembling hands.

All week long Maria asked herself questions without finding answers. Why had her mother lied about eating pork? What was her mother scared of? Why had Angelina called her family a bunch of Jews? Why was Angelina still working in the house after being so nasty? Why hadn't she been punished?

Maria tried to talk about her worries to her nurse before going to bed on Friday night. The señora was brushing Maria's hair with a silver brush. "Why don't we eat pork?" Maria asked.

"Are you still hungry after such a big dinner?" Señora Rodriguez answered with her own question. "A meal fit for a queen —and you act as though you haven't been fed!"

Then Maria said, "Why did Angelina call me a Jew?"

Señora Rodriguez answered, "Because she doesn't have the brains to think of anything else to say."

Maria tried a third time: "Why doesn't Pedro have his book-keeping lesson here tomorrow?"

"What? Do you want me to have to clean another room?"

"Oh, why won't you answer my questions? Ouch!" The brush got caught in a knot in Maria's hair as she tried to pull away. Maria began to cry in frustration. "Leave me alone!" she yelled, throwing herself on the bed. "Leave me alone!" She expected Señora Rodriguez to come over and rub her back. Instead the nurse did as she was told and left the room.

Maria cried herself to sleep with her clothes still on.

She had a hard time sleeping through the night. She kept dreaming the strangest dreams. In one, she was standing with a bunch of Jews—dirty people with horns growing out of their heads. Among them she saw her mother and father, and they also had horns on their heads. Then Maria felt her own head. Oh, horror! There were hard little bumps on either side, and she could feel them growing.

Next in the dream, the Lord Jesus came walking into the crowd. The Jews didn't like him and jumped on him. They nailed him to a cross and laughed at him. "King of the Jews!" they called him. "Look at him now!" Then Angelina, who was also in the dream, pointed at Maria. "And there's the queen! Get her!" All the Jews rushed at Maria, shouting and making horrible faces.

Maria woke up from her nightmare. Her clothes were all damp from her sweat. She jumped out of bed and ran into the hallway to find someone, anyone, who would comfort her.

Outside the windows she could see the daylight breaking. The house was very quiet. Then Maria heard footsteps down below on the tiled floor of the big hall near the front door. She crept to the edge of the staircase and looked down. Her brother, Pedro, was standing by the door, pulling on his cloak. Their mother, still dressed in her sleeping gown, was with him. Maria wondered where Pedro was headed so early in the morning. "To his book-keeping lessons? I thought Momma and Poppa go with him!"

More lies! She was sick of worrying and dreaming and crying. Maria decided to find answers for herself. She ducked back into her room until she heard the front door close and her mother's footsteps disappearing from the hall. Then, quick as a mouse, she dashed downstairs and out the door to follow her brother.

The streets were almost empty, and his black cloak made him easy to see. He walked on and on until Maria's feet began to hurt, and she began to wonder why he wasn't riding his horse. Lucky for her that he wasn't; although Maria knew how to ride, she had never been allowed to take her pony onto the streets by herself. "But I would if Pedro did," she told herself bravely. "Today is not a day for obeying the rules."

Maria made the sign of the cross to protect herself. Pedro was leading her into a part of Toledo where she had never been.

He rested a minute on the edge of the Tagus River, watching the sun's reflections on the water. Maria hid in the doorway of a blacksmith's shop. Pedro then walked one more block and stopped at a stone wall with an iron gate, on which was hanging a piece of parchment. Pedro stopped to read it, then walked through the gate, shaking his head sadly.

Maria had never been to school. There were no public schools in those days, and the private schools, run by the Catholic Church, were only for boys or for girls training to become nuns. However, Doña Flora da Silva had hired a tutor to teach Maria to read, and the message on the parchment was not very long:

To the Jews of Toledo—
The king of Spain, His Royal Highness Ferdinand, com-mands all Jews in the land to accept baptism in the holy waters of the Church or to be banished from the land. After the thirty-first day of July, any unconverted Jew found in Spain will be put to death.

A message from the Inquisition! Why was it hanging on this gate, unless . . . Oh, no! Could it be that Pedro had led her to the *judería* —the Jewish ghetto?

Why, why? Maria could almost hear Angelina's voice, as if Angelina were standing right behind her again, whispering into her ear: "Dirty, secret Jews! You'll burn!"

Maria crossed herself again. "Dear Jesus," she prayed, "say it's not true. They're not Jews, not Jews! Oh, what should I do?" She couldn't run home—not to the Jews! But where else could she run? Her terrible secret would follow her everywhere—even to confession! She had to find out the truth, which meant following Pedro into the ghetto—a brave decision for Maria to make, for she had heard many awful stories about Jews drinking the blood of Christian children. She took a deep breath and ran through the gate. Just inside was a gigantic synagogue, built in the Arabic style, with an onion-shaped roof.

A large crowd of Jewish men and women was standing on the synagogue steps. "What are we to do?" Maria heard one man say. "After so many generations, so many hundreds of years in Spain. Where will we go?"

"Do you know why it's happening?" said another Jew. "Because that rascal Ferdinand is having trouble paying for his wars. He wants every bit of Jewish money in Spain to be in his pocket."

The scene was like Maria's nightmare. There among the Jews she saw Pedro, talking to an old man with a long, white beard. "Pedro!" Maria called out.

"Maria!" Pedro was shocked to see his little sister at the bottom of the steps. "Maria, how in the world did you . . . ?"

"Pedro, why are you *here?*"

"Rabbi," Pedro explained to the old man, "this is my sister. She. . ."

The old Jew smiled at Maria. "Welcome to where your people live, señorita."

Maria crossed herself and ran for the gate. "Maria!" Pedro cried after her.

"Sh," said the rabbi, patting the boy's shoulder. "She must be very afraid."

"But I don't know how she . . ."

"Never mind how," the rabbi said. "Catch her! And teach her!"

Pedro caught up to Maria just outside the gate. "What's wrong with you?" he said angrily, giving her a good shake. "Why don't you speak when the rabbi tells you something?"

"He's a Jew!" Maria screamed. "And so are you!"

Pedro let her go and folded his arms across his chest. "And so are our father and our mother. And so, little sister, what do you think that makes *you*?"

"No!" Maria screamed, stamping her foot. "No, no, no! I never killed Jesus, and I never would!"

"Nor would I," Pedro agreed, "for I never met the man. I hear he was a learned Jew."

"He was the Son of God!"

"We are all sons and daughters of the Almighty," Pedro replied. "Whoa!" He caught her by the arm again. "Don't try to run away, Maria. You can't run from yourself. Tell me what else you have learned about the Jews."

"They kill Christian children!"

"Ah, yes," Pedro teased her, "many times I've seen our father tear apart little Christian babies for supper. . . ."

"He would not!" Maria shouted.

"But why not? He's a Jew!"

"Yes, but . . ."

"Ah!" Pedro said. "So perhaps what the priest has taught you about the Jews is not so true, hm? Or, at least, it's not true about our father."

"Of course not," Maria said. "Poppa wouldn't hurt anyone!"

"What else, then?" Pedro said. "What other stories have you been told about the Jewish people?"

Maria hung her head and sobbed. "They have horns growing on their heads."

"Ah, yes, like bulls," Pedro teased her again. "Our mother, beneath her beautiful head of hair—from which you received the blessing of *your* beautiful hair, Maria—our mother must each day file down the horns growing out of her head."

"No!" Maria cried.

"You mean you don't believe that either?" Pedro said, pretending to be surprised. "Well, what *do* you believe, Maria?"

"I don't know," she whined. "I don't know!"

"Well," Pedro said in a gentle voice, "if you come home with me, you will learn." He took his sister's hand. "From me. From Momma. From Poppa."

Suddenly he yanked Maria into a doorway. Four of the king's soldiers were riding down the street, right outside of the *juderia*. Maria could see the shine of their armor and swords as they passed. Pedro whispered, "You may be afraid of the Jews and of your own family, but you will learn to be more afraid of men like these, Maria. You must learn how to live in secret, how to act like a Christian without believing what they teach, how to lead your Jewish life without being seen. Can you do such things, Maria? Can you keep a secret?"

"I followed you here, didn't I?" she boasted. "You didn't see me until I called you."

Pedro hugged her. "You were always better than I was at hide-and-seek."

"But Angelina knows!" Maria said, suddenly remembering. "Angelina will give away the secret!"

"No, it's too late for her to do that," Pedro said. "Señora Rodriguez's daughter is on her way to Italy, to a quiet convent. She'll make a lousy nun, I'm afraid, but . . ."

"Does the señora have to go with her?" Maria asked fearfully.

"She's a wonderful woman, isn't she?" Pedro said. "And a loving nurse to you. She has known all along that we are secret Jews, Maria. But the señora, you see, believes in what Jesus taught: 'Love thy neighbor'."

"Will she stay with us," Maria asked again, "even without Angelina?"

"I don't know, Maria. She hasn't yet made up her mind. But we'll pray for it, hm?" Pedro said. "Now, let's go home!"

"Home?" Maria groaned. "But I'm so tired! Why didn't you bring your horse?"

"Today," Pedro said, "is the Jewish Sabbath. A Jew does not ride on the Sabbath."

"Then why did you come here to—" Maria still had a hard time saying the word without feeling hateful—"to the Jews?"

"That man who was on the steps of the synagogue with me," Pedro explained, "is a great rabbi. He was teaching me—preparing me to be bar mitzvah."

"What does that mean?"

"It means," he said proudly, "that I am to take my place as a man among the Jewish people—even if I do it in secret! I'm a little old for it, and you, Maria, are young. So we'll learn together."

"With Momma?"

"And with Poppa. Come!"

The Sabbath day had passed into night, into the days of the week. Maria was curled up in her mother's lap in front of a roaring fireplace. She couldn't remember ever being in this room, a hidden room in which Señor Ricardo and Doña Flora da Silva said their Sabbath prayers each week.

For hours they had been telling Maria stories about the Jews. There was the story of a man named Abraham and his wife, Sarah. They had come to another country, and Abraham was scared to tell the king, who liked Sarah, that she was his wife. "Just as we," Señor da Silva told Maria, "are afraid to tell of our real faith." He explained to her that Abraham was the first Jew.

Then there was Queen Esther—"Also a secret Jew," said Maria's mother. "But Esther did not tell her husband, the king, that the Jews were her people until all the Jews were about to be killed by Haman, the villain. When Esther told the king that she was Jewish, the king saved the Jews from Haman."

"But Poppa," said Maria when she heard this, "shouldn't you tell King Ferdinand that *you* are a Jew? Then maybe he wouldn't make all the Jews leave, and Pedro could be bar mitzvah!"

"If I were the king's wife, and not just his tax collector, perhaps

I would," Maria's father said. "But the Inquisition is more power-ful than Haman ever was, so I don't think it would do any good."

"Save your questions," Doña Flora da Silva told Maria, "at least a few of them. We will tell you stories from the Torah every night before you go to bed and on every Sabbath. Soon you will under-stand what it means to be a Jew."

Stories every night! The family together all day every Saturday! Maria began to make the sign of the cross so that her good luck would last. Then she stopped herself, remembering: the sign of the cross was for Christians to make, not for Jews. "But what sign should a Jew make?" she wondered. At that very moment, her mother kissed her.

Commentary

It is interesting that Jews were expelled from Spain in 1492, the very year that Christopher Columbus "discovered" America. Here, in America, our founders built a society in which no one could be persecuted because of religion—no Inquisition, no Mar-ranos. America's founders did not want their new nation to expe-rience the religious oppression found in Spain and in most of Europe. They established the separation of church and state, a constitutional guarantee that all Americans can practice—or not practice—any faith they choose. The First Amendment in our Bill of Rights guarantees this religious freedom. It may be the great-est achievement of American democracy.

"The Truth about Maria" shows the lowest depth in history of relations between Catholics and Jews. The Spanish Inquisition was the product of centuries of official church teaching that Jews were cursed by God for the sin of having "killed Christ." That teaching prepared the ground for discrimination against Jews, who were treated with contempt, frequently compelled to live in special ghettos, and sometimes forced to convert on pain of tor-ture or death. There can be little doubt that one reason Hitler was able to destroy six million Jews in the twentieth century was because the seeds of Jew-hatred had been planted by Christianity for a thousand years.

Only in the past two decades has the Roman Catholic Church taken steps to drain the poison of anti-Semitism from its teachings. The Second Vatican Council, convened in 1962 by Pope John XXIII, resulted in the historic 1965 statement condemning anti-Semitism, denying that Jews killed Christ, and calling upon Catholics to accept Jews and respect Judaism as the faith which gave birth to Christianity. While some Jews said the statement was too little and too late, in truth it marked a real change in Catholic Church doctrine and set the stage for improved Catholic-Jewish relations. The Church set up special departments to strengthen relations with Jewish temples and communities. Now Catholics and Jews are working together in hundreds of communities, learning about each other and cooperating in joint efforts to reverse the nuclear arms race, to feed the hungry, and to house the homeless.

There have been many periods in Jewish history when Jews, like the Marranos of Spain, were compelled to hide their identity out of fear of persecution. In much of Europe during World War II, to be a Jew was itself a crime punishable by death. Many Jews faced the terrible dilemma of professing their faith and facing the gas chambers or trying to pass as Christians. Some desperate mothers saved their children by leaving them with courageous Christian families. Some of these children were baptized and raised as Catholics. In some cases, the Christian "parents" refused to give these children back to their true parents when the war ended. Abraham Foxman, a prominent leader of the Anti-Defamation League, was one of these children. He was raised by a loving Catholic nurse who could not bear to part with him. It took an anguished legal case to return Abe to his original parents. Until that happened, Abe was a modern Marrano.

Even in America, in my generation, when discrimination against Jews was widespread in education, jobs, and housing, many of my friends changed their names (from Berkowitz to Burke or from Greenberg to Green) to hide their Jewish identities. Some Jews even changed the shapes of their noses through plastic surgery in the hope of "passing" as Gentiles. Were these people Marranos? Can their behavior be justified? Measured against the nobility of Jews who have refused to renounce their faith, even in the face of death, these American Jews did not behave very admirably. However, it is hard for us today, living in an open society, to know the frustration caused by anti-Jewish discrimination. Can you imagine how you would feel if the college you wanted to attend accepted only a few Jewish students or if the job you were seeking was closed to Jews?

Yet, even at its worst, anti-Semitism in America was only a pinprick compared to the mistreatment of Jews in other lands. Today, for instance, Jews in the Soviet Union are truly forced to be Marranos. Jews who wish to learn Hebrew in the USSR face harassment and possible imprisonment. Jews who ask to leave the country lose their jobs and apartments and face abuse by neighbors and the secret police. Their children, too, are punished and denied access to colleges and jobs.

The Soviet press, literature, and books generally portray Jews as leeches, parasites, drunkards, even Nazis. Synagogues have been closed down on the outrageous charge that they are dens of thieves and smugglers. Imagine the risks Soviet Jews take when they stand up and proclaim pride in their people! Yet many brave Soviet Jews do openly affirm their Jewishness. While some are lucky and are allowed to leave, most are not. It is therefore not surprising that many other Jews in the USSR behave like modern-day Marranos, afraid to express outwardly the Jewish identity they preserve inwardly.

Even today, you and I could find ourselves in a situation where we, like Marranos, might have to choose whether or not to reveal our Jewish identities. Although we Jews are essentially secure in America, Jews have become targets of radical terrorists like the PLO throughout the world. These groups have declared war on Israel, calling it the "Zionist entity" and claiming the right to destroy it. They think they advance their cause by killing Israelis and Jews at random anywhere in the world.

In June, 1985, a TWA airplane was hijacked in Athens by Moslem extremists and flown to Beirut. There, all the passengers' passports and personal valuables were taken. The hijackers then separated for "special treatment" all those passengers with Jewish-sounding names. Those who were "selected" did not know whether or not they would be killed. (As it turned out, they were all freed after many frantic days of international tension.)

What would you have done in this situation? Would you have pretended to be non-Jewish, as one of the Jewish passengers did? Do you blame him for doing that? I don't. He was dealing with religious fanatics who were crazed by their hatred of Jews.

Strangers in a Strange Land

Three hundred and fifty years ago, New York City was called New Amsterdam. It was a small town owned by Holland, the country that had bought the island of Manhattan from the Indians who lived there. The people of Holland, the Dutch, used the town mainly as a center for fur trapping since animals with valuable furs, like beaver and fox, were plentiful in Manhattan and the surrounding area.

New Amsterdam was established at a time when many European nations were starting colonies in the New World—the world of North and South America—and were competing with each other for power and wealth. Holland, Spain, Portugal, England, France—all of them had colonies and were at war with each other, fighting most of their battles at sea.

For the people living in the world outside of Europe, colonization brought great unhappiness. Indians already living in North and South America were pushed off their land and often were killed by the Europeans. People from Africa were brought as slaves to labor in the colonies. For poor or persecuted Europeans, however, the colonies were an opportunity to start a new life, perhaps with more freedom than they had in Europe.

This was true for the Jews of Spain. As we saw in our last story, Spanish Jews had been forced to become Catholics or leave Spain by 1492. That was the year when Christopher Columbus "discovered" the New World and the countries of Europe began to build their colonies. In fact, Columbus had a few Marranos (secret Jews) with him on his famous voyage. But most of the thousands of Jewish families who were thrown out of Spain could not leave Europe so easily.

For about a hundred years these families wandered far and wide in search of a safe place to live. Some settled in Poland, others in Italy, others in Turkey, and others in the Middle East. Many Jews ended up in Holland, a European country known for its religious freedom. Why hadn't they gone there immediately after leaving Spain? Because Holland itself wasn't independent from Spain and from the Catholic Church until 1581!

Once independent, the Dutch practiced a kind of Christianity called Protestantism. But Dutch Jews were allowed to observe their Judaism openly and still have rights like other Dutch people. Jews were not forced to become Marranos in Holland. Still, some wanted to get away from Europe itself and start a new life, and so they became colonists in the New World.

Five hundred Jews settled in Recife, the capital of Dutch Brazil, in South America. This colony had been captured from Portugal by the Dutch navy in 1630. The five hundred Dutch Jews were therefore joined by many Portuguese Marranos, who were glad to have the Dutch in charge so that they could openly be Jews. They weren't glad for long, however, because in 1654 the Portuguese reconquered Recife. The Dutch Jews and the Marranos were told to get out within three months—or else!

In sixteen ships, the Jewish colonists sailed for Holland or for Dutch colonies. Yet even on the ocean, far from any church or country, the Jews were not safe. One of the ships, with twenty-three Jews aboard, was captured by Spanish pirates; the pirates were then captured by a French warship. After months of wild, dangerous adventures, these twenty-three Jews, both grownups and children, landed safely at New Amsterdam during the first week of September, 1654—just a few days before Rosh Hashanah.

At last they were safe from the Portuguese and the Inquisition. They were safe from pirates. They were safe from the perils of the ocean itself. Still the Jews were not safe because the governor of New Amsterdam, Peter Stuyvesant, a stern man with a wooden leg, simply didn't like Jews.

Stuyvesant wrote back to Holland, to the Dutch West India Company, which was in charge of the colony. He said the Jews would cheat Christians in business, were too poor to support themselves, and were "hateful enemies . . . of Christ." He asked for the company's permission to send the Jews back to Holland immediately.

It took about six months for the Dutch West India Company's reply to reach New Amsterdam. Mail moved slowly in those days, for there were no airplanes to whisk it across the Atlantic Ocean in a day. In the meantime, the Jews waited without knowing if they'd be able to stay. In the meantime, too, they had to sell everything they owned to pay the captain of the ship that had rescued them from the pirates. Peter Stuyvesant had been right about one thing: these Jews were too poor to support themselves without help through their first winter.

Today, hundreds of years later, more Jews live in New York than in any other city in the world. Yet the New York Jewish community began with twenty-three Dutch women, men, and children, waiting for months to find out if New Amsterdam was to be their permanent home.

Dutch New Amsterdam: 1654

Snow was falling on the New World.

For David Levy, age six, it was the first time he could remember seeing snow. In Recife, where he had lived since he was two, there was never any such thing, only heat from the jungle and heavy rains coming in from the ocean. In Amsterdam, Holland, where he had been born, there was snow every winter—but David could hardly remember that far back in his young life.

He sat at the window, staring through the thick glass at Mill Street, which people in town called "Muddy Street." The daylight was starting to fade. In a few minutes it would be time to light the Sabbath candles. David's father, Asser Levy, was sitting behind the boy and smoking a long, whalebone pipe. David's mother, Sara Levy, was there, too, trying to finish sewing a pair of breeches for David while supper cooked in the fireplace. There was only this one room in the house. It was spotlessly clean but had barely any furniture. Nothing hung on the walls except the cooking pots next to the fireplace, the mezuzah on the doorpost, and an old ram's horn—Asser's shofar—on the wall beside the bed.

"Pretty out there, hm?" said Asser to his son. "We're going to have a white Sabbath. Even when we're too poor to give a proper welcome to the Sabbath Bride, the Lord dresses her up for us."

David didn't stir or speak.

"Now, don't let the old winter worry you, my boy," his father went on. "We're going to get through it just fine. By the grace of God we've been given a number of good beaver skins by the people of the church on Winckel Street. Your mother's handy with the needle, so if we don't sell the skins we'll wear them. But we'll be warm, for sure. And there's food and wood for the fire all over this island."

"And who's going to catch the food," said Sara, "while it's running around on four legs in the forest? And who's going to chop the trees for firewood? You're a butcher, Asser Levy. You're not a hunter or a woodsman."

"Well, we've got to be all of those things," Asser insisted. "All of those, and more. We've got to keep ourselves together until Governor Stuyvesant's curse is lifted from our heads and we can live like free Dutchmen."

Hearing this, David turned from the window to look at his father.

"What do you see when you look at me, son?" asked Asser. "You see what the Torah calls 'a stranger in a strange land.' That's what it says about Moses when he had to change from a life of luxury in Pharaoh's palace to the hard life of a shepherd in the wilderness. Do you remember the story I told you—last week's Torah portion?"

David nodded. His eyes were wide and questioning.

"Well, that's how we're living now," his father said. "We're in the wilderness. But remember, David: In the wilderness is where

Moses found wisdom. In the wilderness is where he found the burning bush. . . ."

Sara interrupted her husband. "What's wrong, David? You look like a hungry little bird."

David felt his eyes stinging with tears and quickly stared at the floor. "Why did the governor put a curse on us?" he asked in a low voice.

"Oh, it's not a real curse!" his mother said.

"Not much!" laughed Asser. "Everything we own except our clothes, taken away and sold!"

"That wasn't the governor's fault," Sara said. "That was the captain."

"They're one and the same," he argued. "They say that we Jews drive a hard bargain in business, eh? But they themselves are made of stone."

"And what about the church people who gave us the skins?" Sara pointed out, then said to David: "There are good and bad in every people."

Asser puffed furiously on his pipe, stood and tapped the ashes into the fireplace. "The story of why we Jews are cursed," he answered his son at last, "is a long, long story—thousands of years long. But it comes down to one thing, David: We're cursed because we're smart. And do you know why we're so smart?"

David shook his head.

"We're smart," said his father with another laugh, "because we're cursed."

"Asser!" cried Sara. "Don't speak in riddles! He's upset!"

Asser reached to his tobacco pouch for a refill.

Sara spoke tenderly to David. "What Father is trying to say is that, because our people have no home, we have wandered all over the world. By wandering all over, we have learned many things from wise people all over the world. Because we know so many things, the rulers of the lands where we try to settle are afraid of us and force us to wander again."

"Like Pharaoh did to us in Egypt!" Asser said. "We had to wander for forty years in the desert to be free of him! But at least in the desert there was no snow, hm?" Asser laughed merrily at his joke while Sara began to inspect the stitchery on the breeches. David turned back to his window. He didn't understand what his parents were talking about. All he knew was that he had lost everything—his toys, his friends, his favorite chair—and here the snow was falling and covering up all the places in his new town. "I don't want to wander for forty years!" David thought miserably. "I'll be old by then! I don't care if it's because I'm smart. So what? I'd rather be dumb. Anyway, the Indians are smart. They can hunt and fish and make things and live off the land—and they don't have to wander any place! I'll be an Indian, that's what I'll do. Anything but a Jew!"

His thoughts were very confused, and the confusion made him cry. Sobs shook his little shoulders. The next thing he knew, Sara was at his side, hugging him. "What is it, David?"

He pointed to the window. "I . . . I can't see anything!"

"But what are you looking for?"

"New Amsterdam! The fort! The blacksmith! The . . ."

"Oh, it's all still there, darling," said his mother. "It's all still there. The snow doesn't make it go away. What a silly boy you are!"

"I am not!" He screamed and kicked his feet. "I'm not! I'll stop being a Jew! I'll run away and be an Indian! I won't move any more! I won't!"

Suddenly Asser jumped up from his chair. "Good idea! Let's go find the Indians!" He picked up David and threw him over his shoulder.

"No! Momma!"

"Come on!" Asser shouted. "Outside we go!"

"No! I don't want to!"

"No?" Asser twirled him through the air and landed him on his feet. "Then we'll become pirates, eh?" Asser crouched over and curled his mouth into a horrible sneer. His voice became loud and evil. "And what this pirate likes to do on the Sabbath is to eat little Jewish boys."

David went running wildly across the room, screaming while

his father laughed a wicked laugh. There was hardly any furniture for David to hide behind, but his father moved slowly, like a lumbering giant, while David scooted all over the place. His tears were dry now; he was having great fun.

Even his mother joined in the game. "Look!" She pointed to David's pallet. "There's New Amsterdam! The pirate can't catch you there!" So David ran twice more around his father's legs and then jumped onto his pallet.

Asser came closer and closer to "New Amsterdam." David screamed at the top of his lungs. All at once Asser sank to the floor with a groan. "Hooray!" Sara shouted. "The cannon from the fort sank the pirate ship! Hooray!"

"Hooray!" David cheered, bouncing on his knees.

He wanted to play more, but it was time to greet the Sabbath. Asser picked himself up off the floor and went for his prayer shawl. Sara put away her sewing in a hurry, then lit the Sabbath candles and prayed over the flames. The room became very quiet and peaceful; the air seemed almost perfumed. But for David it meant a return of his loneliest feelings.

He remembered how Shabbat used to be in Recife, where there were so many other Jews. He remembered the wooden synagogue, which his own father had helped to build, and how much fun it was to go there to see everybody dressed up for the Sabbath. And then—even better!—the Levys would have guests to their house for dinner, including other kids like David's friends, Salvatore, Abraham, Joseph, Rebecca. . . .

All gone, now, across the ocean to Holland. . . .

Oh, and the table! The white lace tablecloth, the silver spoons! The shiny, flowered dishes so clean and colorful, ready to be filled with delicious food! All of it, sold here in New Amsterdam to pay the debt to the captain. David's mother still cried about that, sometimes.

"It used to be so pretty," David said with a sniff as they began to eat.

"What was pretty?" asked his father.

"Shabbat."

"In Recife, you mean?"

David nodded and swallowed hard. He didn't want to cry again or see his mother cry.

Asser seemed to understand. He took Sara's hand and reached across the table for David's, too. "It will be pretty again for us, my pretty family. Even more than in Recife. We'll have a big house with lots of china and silver and furniture and toys. And we'll build a synagogue more beautiful than the one in Old Amsterdam itself."

"Why didn't we go *there?*" asked David with a pout.

"Because," his father replied, "I'd rather live in a young land than in an old one. Europe is an old, grouchy man who kicks us out of his garden every few years. Here in the New World there's nobody to kick us out! Nobody except the Indians, perhaps. But if we treat them with respect . . ."

"Everybody else went to Holland!" David complained.

"Yes, and if they ever need to *leave* Holland, as we've had to leave every other country in Europe, they'll be able to come here. We're here to prepare the way for other Jews, David. Just as Joseph did in Egypt. When the famine came, the Hebrew people could go to Egypt, where there was food, because Joseph had prepared the way for them. Do you remember *that* story?"

David frowned as he nodded.

"Besides," Asser went on, "the Jews in Holland are helping us, too. They're going to tell the Dutch West India Company to let us stay here. Some of the Jews in Amsterdam own part of the company, too, so the company will have to listen. And then . . . well, old Governor Stuyvesant will have to step aside, or else we'll kick his one good leg out from under him and he'll fall on his . . ."

"Asser!" Sara scolded her husband. "Don't be cruel. It's the man's heart that matters, not his legs. Remember, Jacob himself had to limp!"

"You're absolutely right, dear. I'm sorry." Asser caught David's eye. "What about you, young man? Do you know what your mother is talking about?"

David nodded glumly. It was the story of Jacob wrestling with God's angel—more Torah! He didn't want to be talking about Bible stories; he felt too frustrated. David threw his wooden spoon onto the table. "Who cares?" he said.

"About Torah?" said his mother in a voice of surprise. "We care! We care because we can learn how to live from Torah, how to live like human beings. It's never the wrong time for learning!"

"Yes, it is!" David whined. "You're just talking and talking about that stuff because there's nobody else to talk to. Who cares about being Jews if there's no such thing as other Jews?"

"But of course there are other Jews!" she said. "All over the world! And when we study, and when we pray, and when we greet the Sabbath, we *are* talking to them."

"No, we're not!" David insisted. "I don't want to talk to them that way. I want to talk to them *here!* Here! Here!" He was nearly in tears again.

"Sh. There are other Jews here, too," said Sara. "There were twenty-three of us on the ship, darling—including your friend Isaac, and Esther, and . . . and most of them live right here on Muddy Street."

"But we never even see them!" David said. "Not really! Only in the street! How come they never come here for Shabbat?"

Asser and Sara looked at each other. Their son was absolutely right. The Jewish families had not been socializing or even praying together very much. "It's because everybody is so poor," Sara said. "We're ashamed of our poverty. Guests for Shabbat must be fed, but we can barely feed ourselves!"

"Those are just excuses," Asser said. "Poor Jews have been getting together to share the Sabbath for hundreds of years. There is no shame on God's holy day. No, it's not shame—it's fear. That's our problem. We're afraid that if we act as Jews or worship as Jews, the Dutch will turn against us."

Sara sighed. "We were so close on the ship in the middle of the ocean," she recalled. "And when the pirates captured us and we thought we might all die . . . and we prayed together, and held one another. . . . Why has all of that changed so much?"

"Because," Asser said with growing anger, "instead of fighting against Peter Stuyvesant's bigotry, we've been surrendering to it! Instead of building our lives here—Jewish lives in a Jewish community, as we did in Recife—we've been hiding like a bunch of Marranos! Well, no more." He stood up. "My family left Spain and Portugal because they refused to be Catholics. They refused to bow to the Inquisition. They wanted to be Jews. And now, look at us, hiding because of one Jew-hater. For shame!"

David slumped in his chair. He was afraid of his father's angry tone, afraid that if it weren't for the Sabbath he might get smacked for whining so much. To David's amazement, Asser gave him a broad, loving smile. "David, my boy, sit up! You're going to be a rabbi someday—perhaps the first rabbi in New Amsterdam! And do you know why? Because you know how to ask the right questions—just like Hillel! Now, come. . . ." He held his hand out to his son. "We're going out for real this time, into that snow. Not to find Indians or pirates, but to find Jews!"

"Asser," Sara cautioned, "it's dangerous outside at night. And you cannot carry a musket on Shabbat."

"A musket?" he said. "Did Moses have such a thing when he went into Pharaoh's court to demand that the Hebrew slaves be set free?"

"There were no Indians in Pharaoh's court," she replied with a smile. Her husband, she saw, was in a grand, dramatic mood.

"Well," Asser said, "some say that the Indians are one of the lost tribes of Israel. Whether this is true or not I can't say—but they are God's children and will not harm us in this mission."

"Oh, so you're on a mission from God?" Sara laughed. "Are you the prophet of New Amsterdam, now? And what will you do for a lamp, O prophet, when you can't carry one on Shabbat?"

Asser threw open the door to the house. The cold air washed in, along with a few snowflakes. "Look out there. The moon is our lamp. And the snow spreads its light everywhere. Besides," he added in a lower voice, "we're not going very far. But enough of your warnings, wife! Put on your beaverskin boots—you're coming with us! And so is this!" Asser took the old shofar down from the wall over his and Sara's bed. "My great-grandfather blew this as he crossed the Spanish border in 1492. My great-grand-parents and my grandfather blew it in a little village in Poland. My parents blew it in the synagogue in Amsterdam. And tonight . . ." Asser slung the ram's horn over David's shoulder. "Tonight we're going to blow the shofar in Peter Stuyvesant's ear!"

It was usually fairly quiet in New Amsterdam at night. The farm animals who by day filled the air with their clucks and squeaks and lowing were inside barns or asleep in the fields after sunset. The hardworking farmers went to bed early, too, so they could get up with their animals in the wee hours of the morning. Shops were closed, and the sounds of hammering and sawing that all day long announced the building of new homes, barns, and fences were vanished. The only noise in town came from the taverns, where fur trappers and traders would sit around getting drunk, talking business, and trading stories—and sometimes trading punches, too.

But the snow made the quiet of the evening feel even deeper, David thought as he and his parents stepped into the crunchy carpet of snow. It made the lamplight in his neighbors' windows look especially warm and cozy; it made the poor houses look no worse than the rich ones. Even Muddy Street looked clean and peaceful, like a sleeping child under a downy white blanket. David looked up at his mother with a smile, then crouched to feel the wet, white crystals, bringing some to his tongue for a taste. "Is the snow kosher?"

His parents laughed and explained that snow is frozen water.

That made David think of their months on the ocean, where everything, all around, had looked the same: blue water, blue sky. This time, however, he wasn't feeling lonely, thinking about his lost friends and things. Instead, David was wrestling with certain thoughts that he tried to express as his parents took his hands and began to stroll with him.

"I think . . . I think if it snowed all the time, then nobody would be different."

"What do you mean, son?" asked Asser. He was impressed to hear his little boy sounding so philosophical.

"I mean . . ." David dropped his father's hand and pointed all around. "Everybody's the same when it's like this. Nobody's poor, everybody's . . . I mean, everything's white, and wet. . . . It's like on the ocean," he said, trying all over again to express his thoughts. "We thought the pirates were going to sink our ship. And so we were all the same. We were all scared. You see, Poppa? Because none of us could swim like the fish. None of us could fly like the seagulls. None of us could get away. We're all just people!"

Asser was very serious as he answered: "It is true that each of us is very alone, and all of us are very much the same, when we face the Angel of Death. The Angel of Death knows every language and listens to none. The Angel of Death doesn't care if you're a pirate or a butcher or a governor, a rich man or a poor woman, a grownup or a child, a scholar or an ignoramus."

David wasn't satisfied. He hadn't meant to talk about dying— that was just an example of what he meant. So he pointed to the moon. "What about that? We're all just like little bugs when the full moon is out."

"And when the sun shines and warms us," said his mother.

"And when the rain falls and fills our wells," said Asser.

"And when we see a cow give birth to a calf."

"And when we see any of God's creations."

"So how come," David asked, "some of us are Jewish bugs, and some of us are Indian bugs, and some of us are Dutch bugs . . . ?"

"If every bug were a bumble bee," his father replied, "would you like that?"

"Uch! No, I hate bees."

"Because they sting you when you put your nose in the wrong flower, eh? But creation is not based upon David Levy's nose! Creation is based on God's wisdom."

"Each kind of bug," Sara explained, squeezing David's hand to get his attention, "does a different kind of work. The bees make the flowers bloom. The worms make the soil good for the farmers. The mosquitos—yes, even those pests!—serve as food for the birds. All these bugs are different—yet they're all bugs!"

"But that's not how it works with people!" David said. "We don't do different kinds of work than other people do, people who aren't Jewish."

"Well," Asser said, "I am a kosher butcher. And my next struggle in New Amsterdam will be to convince the old governor to allow me to open up a business."

David stamped his foot in the snow. "That's not what I mean! You're a butcher! And Momma is a mother! And we're Dutch, right? And we have to wear clothes, right? See? We're just like other people!"

Asser laughed. "That depends upon to whom you talk. Look there." They had just rounded the corner onto Brouwer Street, one block from home. They could see the wall of Fort Amsterdam, which looked out over the harbor. "The men of New Amsterdam stand guard on that wall each night—even when it's snowing," Asser said. "They watch for pirate ships, for Portuguese warships, and for Indian war parties. The Indians might make war, God forbid, because the last governor before Peter Stuyvesant was a damned fool and killed many Indians for no good reason. So we must atone to the Indians, but we must also stand guard to protect ourselves. And that includes us, David, because if you ask an Indian, he'll say that we're Dutch, plain and simple. Our skin color is the color of the Dutch; our clothing is Dutch; and we are visiting the Indians' homeland, with all the rest of the Dutch.

"But those Dutchmen," Asser continued, pointing again to the fort, "will not let your father stand guard with them! I've tried—they turned me away! Why? Why, son? Haven't I got two good eyes in my head? Haven't I got ears that can hear footsteps in the woods and a musket that I can aim as well as the next fellow? Yes, the answers to all my questions are yes. But yes, I'm a Jew! And yes, Governor Stuyvesant thinks there's something different, terribly different, about being a Jew! And yes, as long as Peter Stuyvesant thinks that way, I'll shout at him—Do you hear me, Governor?" Asser was shouting into the night. "I'm a Jew! And I'll stay right here because I'm no worse than you!"

"Asser, please," Sara hushed him. "This will not help our cause. You sound like a drunkard from the White Horse Tavern."

Asser bowed his head. They all began to walk back to Muddy Street.

David knew his father was unhappy and that it was best to be quiet for a while, but he had questions burning inside of him. He tugged his mother's hand. "You said there *is* something different. Like with the bugs . . ."

Sara stood still. "Yes, David. But what's different has nothing to do with our eyes or ears or skin or guns. It has to do with hundreds of years of history—of learning, suffering, wandering. And this is something you can study and study and still never know enough about."

Asser suddenly placed his hands on David's head, warming his little red ears. "It has to do," Asser said in a hoarse voice, "with what's in here, in your head. And maybe . . ." He rubbed David's chest, on the left side. "Maybe there's such a thing as a Jewish heart, too. But these are things that nobody else can see, David. And when someone like Peter Stuyvesant pretends to see our differences, he's doing it only to keep us away from what we deserve to have. We're *all* different, each one of us—but we're all God's children, and we all deserve the same." Then he slipped the shofar over David's head and slung it on his own shoulder.

They continued to walk along Muddy Street. David felt confused again, and his feet were getting cold. "Everyone gets cold feet," he thought, "so we're all the same. But some people hate us, so then we're different. But that means *they* make us different, and that's bad and it's not really true. Okay, now, when an Indian looks at us, we're no different . . . especially when there's a full moon. . . ."

Then his father blew the shofar. Right in the middle of Muddy

Street, standing in the white snow, he blew a note that tingled in David's ear and reached down into his chest. David caught his breath and waited to hear it again. He wanted to hear it again. And again. And again!

His father blew the shofar, even louder. David wondered what the Indians in the woods might think of this sound—some new kind of owl? Some magic spirit? And what about the men standing guard on Fort Amsterdam? Would they be scared, wondering who it was making this great sound? And what about Peter Stuyvesant himself? David laughed out loud. He could just see the governor falling out of bed—no, hiding *under* his bed—because of the sound of the ram's horn.

A window opened right behind where Asser stood. Another opened across the street. A lamp appeared in a doorway. Each was a Jewish home. People began to call to Asser Levy, asking him what was going on. Asser answered none of them but kept blowing the shofar. Slowly but surely, every Jew on Muddy Street appeared at a window or doorway. At last Asser lowered the ram's horn and spoke.

"Once upon a time a Jew named Joshua blew the shofar, and the shout of the Jewish people made the walls of Jericho fall. Well, here in New Amsterdam, the walls of Jericho are standing once again to keep us out! I say it's time we all shouted!"

David worried that the people were going to shout at his father, who looked like a crazy prophet, with snow all over his hair. But the first voice belonged to Mr. Moses Lucena, the father of David's friend Isaac. "Blessed art Thou, O Lord of the universe, who has given of His wisdom to human beings." Then Mr. Lucena stepped out into the snow and embraced David's father. "Good Sabbath, Asser Levy," he said. "A good Sabbath."

* * *

On April 26, 1655, a letter from the Dutch West India Company arrived in New Amsterdam. It instructed Governor Peter Stuyvesant to permit the Jews to stay there.

Asser Levy went on to open a kosher butcher shop, to stand guard atop Fort Amsterdam, and to win full rights of citizenship—all of which he had to fight for, with patience and strength.

Commentary

Jews came to America as "strangers." In this story we see how the first Jews had to fight even for the right to remain and practice their religion. But now, more than three centuries later, Jews are deeply integrated and legally secure in America. America is a nation different from all others in which our ancestors settled. Everywhere else, even in societies where we lived for centuries, Jews were "on the edge," facing discrimination and ready to flee as soon as a king, a church, or any ruler turned against us. But in America, a land of immigrants, we became full citizens, protected by the Constitution and Bill of Rights, documents of freedom unique in the world.

You and I do not see ourselves as strangers in this land. We do not live, as our ancestors did, with luggage packed, waiting for the next pogrom, the next anti-Semitic edict, the next expulsion. Nor must we surrender our Jewishness in order to be accepted as Americans. In politics, education, literature, the arts, business, and charity, we Jews have made vast contributions to the grandeur of America—contributions that far exceed our small numbers, five and a half million of two hundred and fifty million Americans.

Yet even in America, vigilance is the price of freedom. Despite America's separation of church and state and historic traditions of religious liberty, there are powerful extremist groups seeking to make America strictly a fundamentalist, Christian country and to undermine the guarantees of the Constitution. If these groups succeed, we Jews might once again be strangers in our land.

Like Asser Levy and his fellow Jews, we must be alert to resist efforts to "Christianize" America. We therefore oppose all efforts to mandate prayer in public schools, to erect religious symbols (Christian or Jewish) on public property, or to impose a religious test for public office. This may mean taking unpopular positions and exposing ourselves to hatemongers and kooks, but it is our central role in America to preserve individual liberty and democratic values that are the essence of America—as they are the essence of Jewish ethics.

Fortunately, the truth about anti-Semitism in the United States is that, despite occasional incidents, it has been declining for at least forty years. The best proof of this is in our political system. In 1985 there were eight Jews in the United States Senate and twenty-eight Jews in the House of Representatives. Most of these legislators did not come from strongly Jewish districts or states. Senator Howard Metzenbaum of Ohio, for instance, was re-elected in a state that was less than two percent Jewish. He and other Jewish politicians are proud and assertive in their Jewish identities, but that does not seem to hurt them at the polls. Moreover, Jews, more than any other ethnic group, are very involved in politics, raising money, working for candidates, and voting in large numbers in primaries and general elections. So how anti-Semitic can America be?

Yet there is anxiety among American Jews about anti-Semitism. Opinion polls show that Jews consider non-Jewish Americans more prone to anti-Semitism than they truly are. Clearly, the "gut" anxiety we feel has more to do with the long history of anti-Semitism than with the actual present reality. Does that mean we are oversensitive about anti-Semitism? Maybe—but with the Holocaust so very recent, our nervousness is not surprising. Still, it does cloud our judgment from time to time. One result is that we frequently overreact to a given incident—a politician criticizing Israel, for example—and confuse legitimate differences of opinion with anti-Semitism.

Often there is an age factor involved. Older Jews have "thin skins" on Jewish issues and are very sensitive about anti-Semitism —sometimes mistakenly. Many young Jews, on the other hand, have never experienced violent anti-Semitism. They tend to think their parents and grandparents are touchy, if not fanatical, on these matters.

One way of putting anti-Semitism into perspective is to compare the situation of American Jews with that of black Americans. Blacks have suffered enormous cruelty in this country, and discrimination against them still occurs daily. Hundreds of blacks were lynched in this country before the power of law was finally mobilized against such racism. By contrast, in American history, only one Jew was ever the victim of such horror. His name was Leo Frank. On April 28, 1913, in Atlanta, Georgia, this young Jew was arrested and charged with the murder of Mary Phagan, a fourteen-year-old Christian girl who worked for him. On August 23, 1913, he was found guilty of the crime. His trial was a farce, and it became clear to much of America that an innocent man was being framed because he was a Jew. There was a tremendous protest and outcry to save Leo Frank's life. However, when Governor John M. Slaton of Georgia, an honest and brave man, changed the death sentence to life imprisonment, his own life was threatened by howling mobs. The governor had to be protected by the Georgia militia and smuggled out of the state in the dead of night. Meanwhile, a vigilante committee in the hometown of the slain girl ordered all Jews to leave town. Leo Frank was transferred to a prison camp, where a fellow convict slashed his throat, almost killing him. On August 16, 1915, a blood-thirsty mob, shrieking anti-Jewish slogans, dragged Frank from the jail and lynched him.

Far from being ashamed of this act, Georgians rewarded those who condemned Leo Frank. Hugh Dorsey, the prosecutor, was elected governor, and Tom Watson, the violently anti-Semitic politician and publisher who had fanned the flames of anti-Jewish hatred, was elected to the United States Senate.

This was a dark chapter in American anti-Semitism. Seventy years later Atlanta would become one of America's most liberal cities, with Andrew Young, a black, defeating Sidney Marcus, a Jew, in the mayoral election. Meanwhile, a campaign continues to clear the name of Leo Frank and to achieve a retroactive pardon.

In fact, James Conley, a janitor at the National Pencil Company, which had been owned by Leo Frank's uncle and where Frank was manager, has been identified as the actual killer. Could such an anti-Semitic episode as the Leo Frank case occur in America today?

The Slave Boy

F rom 1861 to 1865, America fought a civil war—a war between the Northern states, which called themselves the
"Union," and the Southern states, which called themselves
the Confederate States of America or the "Confederacy." One of
the main causes of the war was the question of slavery. In the
South, many white people owned black slaves; in the North, most
people were against slavery.

The city of Baltimore, Maryland, was located between the
Union and the Confederacy. While Maryland fought on the
Union side in the war, there were many people in Baltimore who
owned slaves and agreed with the Confederacy.

In a city of about 200,000 people, there were approximately
7,000 Jews, mostly new immigrants who had come to America
after 1850, from Germany, Hungary, and Austria. Among them
was Rabbi David Einhorn, who had come from Germany in 1855
and was one of the few Reform rabbis in America at that time.
Rabbi Einhorn opposed slavery and often spoke strongly against
it, from his pulpit and in *Sinai,* the monthly journal that he published.

This is the story of how anti-Semitism taught a young Jewish
boy in Baltimore to "take sides" on the issue of slavery.

Baltimore, Maryland: 1861

Union soldiers were coming to Baltimore! Hundreds, maybe
thousands, of them! This very Sunday!

Hank (Hiram) Simpson was sitting in Rabbi David Einhorn's study, waiting for his Hebrew lesson. On the rabbi's desk was a copy of a German-language journal. Hank knew German, the language that his parents spoke, even better than he knew English —and much, much better than he knew his Hebrew! So he was very excited by what he read on the front page.

Union soldiers were coming to Baltimore! Sunday!

He knew that many of the grownups in the Har Sinai Congregation would be upset by the news. This new President Abraham Lincoln, they would grumble, seemed to be ready to go to war just because he didn't like slavery. But never mind Old Abe Lincoln, Hank thought. Never mind whether slavery was bad or not. He just wanted to see the soldiers march through town, even if that meant a little sneaking around. He wanted to see those men in their uniforms; hear a thousand marching boots; look closeup at the swords, guns, and cannon; and maybe get a couple of bullets from a sergeant or even a captain!

Sneaking around was not going to be easy, however. It was the Passover season, and every person in every family in the congregation was busy preparing for the holiday. Most of the adults seemed nervous and were stricter than usual with their kids. Hank's parents, Meyer and Bertha Simpson, were nagging him to study, study, study, for in two months he would be bar mitzvah. It seemed to Hank that whenever he went out of his house he had to explain to his mother exactly where he was going and why he wasn't studying.

Even this morning, on his way to his lesson at the rabbi's house, Hank had been questioned by his parents. Where was he going? How long would he be gone? Was he prepared for his lesson? What else did Rabbi Einhorn talk about with him? Hank's father actually seemed angry at the rabbi. "Rabbi David Einhorn," he said to his wife, "should just give Hiram his lessons and leave politics to the politicians. Why should a Jewish leader stick his nose into this slavery business? The enemies he's making are sure to give us *all* a headache!"

Enemies? Who didn't like Rabbi Einhorn, Hank wondered.

Sure, the rabbi had received a couple of nasty letters from people who believed in slavery—but those people were too cowardly even to sign their names to their letters! So what if Rabbi Einhorn felt like talking against slavery! "This is a democracy," Hank thought. "The rabbi can say anything he wants to say. It's a free country."

Then Hank reminded himself: Half the country was not so free. Half the country—including his own city of Baltimore—lived on the labor of slaves. "Oh, but never mind about slavery and Abe Lincoln and all that stuff," he thought. "Who cares anyway?" Hank had enough to worry about with his bar mitzvah studies. He couldn't concentrate, not as long as that journal on the rabbi's desk kept reminding him: soldiers! In Baltimore! Hundreds, maybe thousands!

Hank pushed the journal aside. Underneath it he found a daguerreotype of Rabbi Einhorn. It showed the rabbi wearing a yarmulke, holding a Hebrew book of psalms. "Oh, I better get to work on *my* Hebrew," Hank worried out loud. But he couldn't take his eyes off that picture. "Funny," he thought, "but those dark eyes . . . and those hollow cheeks . . ." The rabbi, Hank realized, looked a lot like President Lincoln!

Hank got to work, carefully tearing little bits of paper to make a beard and tophat, just as Abe Lincoln wore. He lay the paper cutouts on top of the daguerreotype and . . . Presto! There was Old Abe, holding a Hebrew book of psalms. But then, uh-oh! Hank felt a hand on his shoulder. Rabbi Einhorn had come into the study, and Hank hadn't even noticed!

He expected to get a sharp scolding. Instead the rabbi saw what Hank had done to his picture and laughed. "Look at that!" he said in German. "Is that what most of my congregation thinks—that I'm President Lincoln's twin brother? But Lincoln has an army to do his will, and what have I got? I'm an anti-slavery Jew in a town full of gentile slaveholders!" The rabbi sighed and pulled a chair alongside of Hank. "Let's get to work, Hiram. Let it not be said that President Lincoln's Jewish twin can't produce Baltimore's finest bar mitzvah!"

Hank began to read his Hebrew lesson out loud. He could tell right away that Rabbi Einhorn was not himself. The rabbi was not correcting any of Hank's mistakes, nor was he giving his usual words of encouragement. "Funny," Hank thought. "I'm usually the one who can't concentrate." Rabbi Einhorn began to tap his fingers impatiently on the desk. Hank stumbled over an easy word, then glanced into the rabbi's face. "I'm sorry about the picture," Hank mumbled. "The beard and the hat will come off, there's no glue. . . ."

"Ach, I'm worrying you, am I?" said Rabbi Einhorn. "Just as the Know-Nothings are worrying me!"

"What are the Know-Nothings?" Hank asked, afraid that the rabbi was talking about him.

Rabbi Einhorn gently closed the boy's book. "Let me give you another kind of lesson, Hiram. There is more to being a Jew than the Hebrew alphabet. Do you remember, a few years ago—you were very young—we had in Baltimore a group who would scream and holler against foreigners?"

Hank shook his head.

"They were called the 'Know-Nothings,' " the rabbi explained. "They were against all immigrants coming to America, especially the Irish Catholics who were coming in great numbers. The Know-Nothings became very popular in this town of ours. They even got elected to office! But meanwhile they were beating people up on the streets, burning their stores, and for what? For being different, for having a different religion and different customs. What a bunch! They made me so angry, Hiram! I was just an immigrant myself—you know, your family came only the year before I came. But I knew from the start that America's generosity to strangers like me was what made this country great. So I spoke against the Know-Nothings, with all my strength. Many Jews warned me to keep quiet, not to call attention to ourselves. But I would not keep quiet. I could not! And it was the Know-Nothings who disappeared from Baltimore, not I!"

Hank nodded shyly. The rabbi seemed to be making a sermon just for him.

"But now again," Rabbi Einhorn continued, "the Know-Nothings have come, in new clothes, with a new face—the face of the slaveholder! And again there are Jews warning me, 'Don't say anything about slavery, Rabbi.' 'Rabbi, don't make trouble.' 'They'll call us Christ-killers, they'll say we have horns on our heads.' These Jews don't seem to understand that the only way to stop prejudice against the Jews is by opposing *all* injustice, no matter what names you're called!"

Hank shrugged, not knowing what to say. These were things for grown men to talk about, he thought, not for kids.

The rabbi seemed to know what Hank was thinking. "You're still a boy, Hiram," he said, "but soon you'll be bar mitzvah. It's time for you to think about these things. Disagreements are not new to the Jews of our city. I'm sure that your father, who's very active in our synagogue, often talks about the bitter brawls that we, the Reform, have with the Orthodox. When we began seating women and men together at Har Sinai, as equals, instead of exiling the women up near the ceiling—'Heavens!' cried the Orthodox. 'This Einhorn is corrupting our Judaism.' Well, the words I used for them were not so pretty either."

Hank nodded. He could remember when his mother had warned him: "If I ever catch you using the insults that these learned men are using for each other, young man, you'll feel the back of my hand!" Still, there was nothing in Reform Judaism that came between Hank and his friends in the Orthodox congregations. "Kids just know how to get along," he thought.

Rabbi Einhorn leaned an elbow on his desk and cradled his head in his hand. "We aren't getting much work done, are we? Still, I'll give you some work to do at home. I want you to ask your father, Meyer Simpson, why it is that he will defend the equality of women in the synagogue but is fearful to defend the equality of the black race."

Hank grew pale. "I . . . I can't ask him that," he stammered.

"Why not? Don't you speak to your father?"

"Because . . ." Hank was thinking again of what his father had said this very morning about Rabbi Einhorn "sticking his nose into this slavery business." Meyer Simpson, Hank realized, was one of the Jews about whom the rabbi was complaining.

"Well?" said Rabbi Einhorn.

"We don't talk about that kind of stuff!" Hank said.

Suddenly the door to the study opened. Hank was very happy to be interrupted. In came Mordechai Cohen, the father of Hank's buddy, Morty. He was very angry. "Excuse me, Rabbi, but please have a look." He slapped a newspaper onto the desk. "Right here," he said, poking his finger at an article. "It says that the Jews own *all* the businesses in Baltimore and are forcing customers into the poor house. It calls for a campaign to drive Jews out of business instead. Damn Catholics!" he grumbled, for the newspaper was a German Catholic one.

"Never mind cursing them," Rabbi Einhorn advised. "Let's *reply* to them instead." He nodded to Hank. "Please excuse us, Hiram."

Hank scooped up his books and ran.

Sitting between his father and mother at services at Har Sinai, Hank came up with a plan for sneaking away to see the soldiers. During the service, Rabbi Einhorn had read aloud the anti-Semitic article that Mordechai Cohen had brought to him. Rabbi Einhorn had then announced that, in reply to the article, he had written a special essay that would appear in the new issue of *Sinai* on Sunday.

"Sunday?" Hank thought. "That's the day that the soldiers are coming." Then the plan bit him like a bug. He and his friends would tell their parents that, on Sunday morning, they were going to sell copies of *Sinai,* to help fight anti-Semitism in Baltimore. "And we'll do it," Hank thought, "at least a few copies, so that we won't be telling a lie. After we've sold them, we can hurry to see the soldiers."

When services ended, Hank tested out his idea with his parents. "With these soldiers coming to town," Bertha Simpson worried, "there may be all kinds of fights in the street."

"I won't sell any where they're marching," Hank promised.

His mother was not satisfied. "I don't even want you to set foot where they're marching!"

Then Meyer Simpson spoke up. "I suppose Hiram will soon be a man," he said to his wife, "and as a man he has a responsibility to help defend the Jewish community. Let him bring the rabbi's article to the Jews of other congregations and even to the Gentiles. But, young man," he added, "that means extra study of your lessons."

"Aw, what about my day of rest?" Hank whined.

"You'll take off your shoes while you study," Meyer said. "Remember, it is always a mitzvah to read the holy books."

While his parents chatted with their friends on the steps of Har Sinai, Hank ran around telling his friends about his plan. When he returned to his parents' side, Rabbi Einhorn was waiting to congratulate him. "I'm glad to see that our little conversation had some effect on you," the rabbi said.

For a moment, Hank felt ashamed. He knew he wasn't being especially brave or good—he was just getting to do what he wanted to do. He hadn't been thinking about slavery or prejudice —only about the soldiers, their sea of blue uniforms.

After a while, however, the attention began to rub off on him, and Hank began to think of himself as an important person. But there was so much for him to do! He would have to pick up the copies of *Sinai* from the printer. He would have to lug them in his wagon to his friends and then to wherever they were going to sell them. He'd have to wave them like flags to attract customers. He'd have to make sure he had change to give. He'd have to be in charge of the other kids to make sure they were honest and did their work. It was like being a general in the army! General Hank Simpson, leading his Jewish troops through Baltimore! Forward, march!

Only seven kids were waiting for him on Bolton Street when Hank came puffing along on Sunday morning with his wagon full of the copies of *Sinai*. They paid no attention to their general, either, for they were all listening to an argument between Hattie Cohen,

Morty's older sister, and Ruben Nachman. Ruben was an Orthodox kid whose family owned three black slaves.

As Hank stood still to catch his breath, he heard Hattie say, in a mixture of English and German: "Why don't you be my slave for one week and see how it feels, Ruben? Come on, I dare you! It's Passover, and the Haggadah says we should each feel as if we've personally been freed from slavery. So I'll give you a real taste of slavery! And the first thing I'll do is sell your slaveholding daddy down the river to New Orleans!"

"Drop dead, Hattie Cohen," Ruben retorted with a thick German accent. "I'm not a nigger."

"You may not be a nigger, smarty, but the Gentiles don't think much of you as a Jew either. You may have white skin—except that you never wash your face—but to the Gentiles you're nothing but a Christ-killing Jew, no matter how many slaves your daddy buys."

"What's this all about?" Hank asked Morty.

"Ah, my sister started arguing about the usual thing, you know —slavery, the war. . . ."

"Hey, you two," Hank called to them. "Why don't you leave politics up to the politicians? You can't vote anyway. Come on, we've got work to do with these papers before we can see the soldiers."

"Why don't you grow up, Hank Simpson?" Hattie scowled at him. "Who cares about your soldiers? There are Negro children and they're slaves, aren't they? We kids have got to stick up for each other."

"And you, Hiram?" Ruben taunted Hank. "Are you going to stick up for the niggers?"

"Maybe I'll just stick my fist down your throat," Hank growled, even though Ruben was older and bigger.

"And I'll help him!" Hattie volunteered, making fists.

Even Morty thought his sister was getting a little too rough in her talk. "Hattie," he said in German, "girls aren't supposed to talk like that."

"Girls aren't supposed to talk like that," she mimicked him in a whining voice. "Maybe that's another reason why I hate slavery! We're just like the Negroes, we girls—we're not allowed to do a thing except work our fingers to the bone!"

"Please," Hank pleaded, "Can't we go and get rid of these papers and then watch the soldiers?"

Solomon Rosenwald, a younger boy from Har Sinai, shook his head. "Hattie says there's going to be big trouble when the soldiers come."

"What kind of trouble?" said Hank.

Hattie pointed at Ruben. "People like his father are going to make a riot. They want Baltimore to join the Confederacy so they can keep their slaves instead of setting them free. Just like the Pharaoh did—and look at what happened to him!"

"My father is planning nothing." Ruben blustered.

"He is too!" Hattie said.

"You're a liar!"

"Oh, yeah? Let's go down to Slatter's place—that's where they're all going to meet. I bet your daddy will be there."

"He will not!"

"Will!"

"Will not! My father never goes to Slatter's place."

Mr. Slatter was a slave trader. Behind his office on Pratt Street was a yard where the slaves were penned like animals behind high fences during the day. There was also a building with two floors and with bars on the windows, where the slaves were locked up at night. The men who bought from Slatter came from Southern states such as Louisiana and Mississippi, where the slaves they bought were made to work on tobacco and cotton farms called "plantations."

The white people of Baltimore, Jews and Gentiles, owned more than 20,000 black slaves. Still, nobody liked Slatter's business with its tough-talking, tobacco-spitting customers. Even Ruben's father had warned his children never to go near the slave pen. "We take good care of our Negroes," Mr. Nachman liked to say, and he hated to be reminded by Slatter's business of how cruel slavery actually was. At Slatter's place, black children were sold out of their mother's arms. Black men and women were chained so they could not run away and were ferociously whipped if they tried to resist.

"We can't go to Slatter's place," Hank said.

"Why not, Hank Simpson?" Hattie asked. "Just because your mother told you not to? She told you not to go see the soldiers, didn't she? But for that you'll even do some work, lugging those papers around. You'll work like a mule, but you won't do any work with your head!"

"What do you mean?" Hank wasn't sure if Hattie was insulting him or not.

"I mean just what I say. When you stick a carrot in front of a mule, he'll eat it, but he won't know where it came from. So he can't grow his own carrots. But people can because we're supposed to know how to *think*. . . ." Hattie tapped her head and wrinkled her nose at Hank.

"Aw, who wants to stand around listening to you?" he said. "Come on, everybody! Let's get going with these papers!"

"I bet you haven't even read the rabbi's article, have you?" Hattie said.

"Well, no," Hank confessed. "Not yet."

"Why not? How are you going to go selling something that you haven't even looked at? See, that's what I mean about you, Hank. You're like that mule. You're going to go stare at the soldiers, but you won't think about *why* they're coming to Baltimore, *why* maybe there's going to be a war. And then tonight you'll go to your seder, but you won't think about what Passover *means*—that we all deserve to be free."

"Aw, how do you know so much?" Hank said.

"They may not let me be bar mitzvah like you because I'm a girl," Hattie replied, "but I study a lot more than you, I bet."

"Listen to this one!" Ruben sassed her. "She's a scholar!"

"I didn't say that!" Hattie barked. "But I am a Jew, which is more than I can say about any of you."

"Foo, what are you talking about?" Ruben said. "You are crazy."

"I'm talking about that mule again," Hattie said. "A mule can't be a Jew because he can't think. He can't think about what it means to be Jewish. Without thinking, he's just a jackass."

They were all quiet, now, trying to figure out Hattie's meaning. "Come on," she challenged Ruben again, "let's go down to Slatter's place. Then we'll see if you don't choke on your food at your seder tonight!"

"That Hattie Cohen," Hank thought as he stood, at last, watching the soldiers on parade. "That Hattie Cohen put some kind of spell on me." He didn't believe this, of course. Hank was too educated to be superstitious. Still, ever since Hattie Cohen had opened her mouth to him, nothing looked the same any more.

The soldiers, for instance. There were a lot less of them than Hank had hoped to see, and they weren't at all the handsome giants in clean uniforms with shiny buttons that Hank had daydreamed about. They were just plain guys—they could have been the older brothers or fathers of Hank and his friends. They all looked tired, dusty, and maybe a little scared. Yet they were heroes to Hank—not heroes from a storybook, but real-life heroes, because they were marching for a good idea: an end to slavery.

"Slavery! Since when do I care so much about slavery?" Hank thought. But he knew the answer, and the answer was Hattie. She had led them all to Slatter's place. Ruben's father wasn't there, and Ruben kept saying, "You see? I told you! I told you!" But none of the kids paid much attention to Ruben when they saw what was going on there.

The yard was packed with black men and women. The slave-traders were strolling outside the fence. They would point out to Mr. Slatter the slaves they wanted to "inspect." Hank saw three of the white men poking at a black woman, opening her mouth to look at her teeth, squeezing parts of her body, laughing in her face, and acting so horribly that Hank had to look away in shame.

His eyes fell on a black boy who was pressed against the fence on the inside. The boy was also watching the terrible inspection, and his eyes were blazing with hatred for the slave traders. But those fires were flooded with tears when one of the white men called Slatter over to bargain about a price for the woman. "That must be the boy's mother!" Hank realized, and he felt his own eyes stinging with tears.

Never before had he seen a black person cry. For Hank it was like seeing the burning bush that Moses saw in the wilderness, the bush that burned and burned without turning to ash. It was like hearing the voice of God, saying, "Go down to Pharaoh and tell him, 'Let my people go!'" Hank wasn't sure just where to find his Pharaoh. He only knew that he felt sadder than he had ever felt before.

He was angry, too. He wanted to start arguing with anyone and everyone, just the way Hattie Cohen or Rabbi Einhorn would do. He felt hungry to know more, to understand more, to take sides in all those grownup discussions about slavery and Abe Lincoln and whether there would be a war between the states. He wanted to ask Rabbi Einhorn a million questions at their next bar mitzvah lesson; he wanted to tell the rabbi that he, Hank Simpson, cared about slavery.

He wanted not only to ask the Four Questions at his family's seder that night, but to answer them, as Rabbi Einhorn could do, with words about freedom. And then, Hank imagined, he would open the door for Elijah the Prophet—and in would walk that young black boy with the burning eyes, that boy who had become a man by watching his mother being sold.

Hattie had been right about something else, too. A large gang of men, some with clubs, some with guns, were gathering in front of Slatter's office. One of them spotted Ruben's yarmulke and called to him, "Hey, Jew-boy, what are you doing around here looking at our niggers?"

Ruben trembled and said, "I . . . we . . . we're on our way to see the soldiers."

The man pounded the stick he was carrying into the palm of his hand. "So are we, Jew-boy, so are we." He and his gang laughed. To Hank they sounded like barking dogs.

The kids quickly walked away. Hank was slower because he had to pull his wagon. He saw Hattie lingering with ready fists. Hank grabbed her by the arm and yanked her along. "C'mon," he said, "you're too smart to get your head broken."

So now they were standing on Baltimore Avenue, a wide boulevard down which the soldiers were marching in rows of ten across. The sights, smells, and sounds of Slatter's slave market stuck to Hank like cotton balls to clothing. "What should we do?" he said to Hattie. "Those men will be coming here any minute. Who can we warn?"

Hattie shook her head. "Nobody, probably. The sheriff is a slaveholder himself, so he won't do anything. In fact, my father right now is at the rabbi's house, with some other men, to protect the Einhorns. The sheriff said he won't do it."

"Protect them?" Hank said. "Why do *they* have to be protected?"

"Because Rabbi Einhorn is a brave man!" Hattie squinted at Hank. "Don't you understand yet? Here." She snatched a copy of *Sinai* from Hank's wagon. "Read the article he wrote. It tells the whole story."

The soldiers were still filing past, but Hank wasn't watching them anymore. "This is not only an article to defend the Hebrew people of Baltimore from slander and abuse," Rabbi Einhorn's article began. It continued:

> Any educated person whose eyes are not clouded by hatred can see that what is written about the Jews is untrue. But if the Jews are not, in fact, what the Jew-haters say we are, is it not possible that the Negro race, too, has been the victim of lies?
>
> If the Jews, in fact, do not have horns (which any good doctor will tell you) . . . if the Jews, in fact, are not all cheats (as any satisfied customer of a Jewish business will tell you) . . . if the Jews, in fact, are like any people, full of good and bad—if all of this is so, then is it not possible

that the Negro, like the Jew and like the Gentile, has a mind and a heart?

Does the black slave woman not feel pain in her heart when her child is torn away and sold?

Does the black slave man not feel pain in his heart when he is helpless to defend his wife against misuse by the white master?

No, this is not an article to defend the Hebrew people of Baltimore from anti-Jewish slander. This, instead, is an attempt to turn the fight against this particular brand of hatred into a bigger fight, a fight against all the lies that make us hate one another. This is an article against hate.

Our America of the future will not tolerate slavery or prejudice. Our America of the future will be true to the words of the Declaration of Independence: All are created equal!

Some of the words were hard to pronounce, yet Hank understood as soon as he thought again of the slave boy whose mother had been sold. "Yes," Hank thought, "he was a boy like me, with a mind and a heart."

Suddenly a shout went up along the street. The men from Slatter's place were attacking the soldiers, shouting, "Nigger-lovers! Nigger-lovers!" Many others of the people of Baltimore had joined the mob.

Hank looked at Hattie with tears in his eyes. "What can I do, Hattie?" he pleaded. "Should I go to the rabbi's house?"

"You're too young," Hattie said. "And anyway, I thought you didn't care."

"Oh, I do care," Hank swore. "I care a lot."

* * *

Three days later, the print shop that had printed Rabbi Einhorn's journal was smashed and burned by the mob. The rabbi, for the sake of his family's safety, was forced to leave Baltimore and go north to Philadelphia. He never returned, for his congregation was too afraid of his outspoken views on slavery.

The Civil War that everyone feared broke out soon after Passover. It lasted four years, and when Hank turned sixteen, he joined the Union army and fought against slavery.

———

Commentary

Were you shocked to learn that there were Jews in America who owned slaves, and that many Jews saw no conflict between slavery and Judaism? Was it hard for you to believe that a rabbi had to flee for his life because he had the courage to speak out against slavery?

In New York City, Rabbi Morris Raphall, a famous rabbi of his day, preached sermons arguing that Jews *should* support slavery because, after all, Jews owned slaves in biblical times! He was no more typical of the American rabbinate than was the brave-hearted abolitionist, Rabbi David Einhorn. Most rabbis simply kept quiet, hoping not to get involved in the controversy. Remember, during that time there were only 160,000 Jews in all of America, most of them recent "greenhorns" from Germany and other European countries—new immigrants desperate to make a living for their families and gain acceptance in the New World. Few owned slaves, but few felt secure enough to take public stands on the issue that was tearing the nation apart.

However, a century later—when the great civil rights revolution came to a boil in the 1960s—American Jewry was no longer a minor spectator, watching events as young Hank and his friends had done in Baltimore in 1861. In the 1960s, the controversy was not over slavery but racial segregation and discrimination. Again, the nation was being tested and torn apart by the issue of human rights for blacks. Could they register to vote? Could they eat in the same restaurant, go to the same hotel, attend the same school as whites? As in our story, hate-filled racists went wild, blowing up black churches and threatening the lives of blacks who demanded equal rights and justice. Cowardly segregationists put on white hoods and joined the Ku Klux Klan to terrorize blacks and their supporters.

Martin Luther King, Jr., a young black minister from Montgomery, Alabama, spoke up against the sin of racism and touched the conscience of the entire nation. As leader of an aroused black community, he also inspired millions of non-blacks to step forward and work for equal justice.

Among those who stood beside Martin Luther King, Jr., in the greatest moral struggle since the Civil War were many Jews from all over the United States. Many were young, of high school and college age. Many came from the North, traveling to the dangerous communities of Mississippi and Alabama to work for black rights at great personal risk. Many were jailed; some were beaten by the hatemongers of the Deep South.

In 1964, three young participants in the struggle against racial segregation—two Jews and a black—were murdered in Mississippi by hoodlums of the Ku Klux Klan, some of whom were local sheriffs. Andrew Goodman and Michael Schwerner died with their black friend James Chaney and were buried together in the brown hills of that state, martyrs to the cause of racial justice.

Thus, while the fight against slavery in the 1860s involved few Jews, the fight against racial segregation in the 1960s involved many. Why the difference?

By 1960 Jews had grown to a community of six million—three percent of the total population of America—and we played a role far beyond our numbers. No longer an immigrant community, we were secure in American democracy and well organized in numerous, effective organizations. We knew that *our* freedom depended upon freedom for all other minorities in America, and we had the strength to speak out and take a stand.

Not all Jews agreed. It was as difficult for Jews in the Deep South to be pro-black as it must have been for Hank's dad in Baltimore in 1861. However, the large Jewish organizations made no secret of their belief that Judaism stands for equal rights among all of God's children and that racism is a sin against the God who created humankind. Many rabbis became deeply involved in the civil rights movement, setting the example for other Jews.

Of course, there were Jews who, like Meyer Simpson in our story, said that the anti-Semites would be aroused if Jews spoke out against racial discrimination. This was true. The haters did come out of the woodwork. Several synagogues were bombed. Rabbis and congregants alike were often threatened. But would it have been safer for Jews to keep silent and pretend to be neutral? In fact, a few of the synagogues that were bombed actually *had* kept silent in the controversy! Even if standing up to injustice did increase the danger of anti-Semitism, would it have been right for Jews to duck the moral issue that Rabbi Einhorn bravely confronted a century before?

Actually, one of the most important lessons we learn from our history in America is that the only effective way to fight anti-Semitism is to fight for justice for all peoples. Jews cannot be secure if any people can be treated as inferiors, as blacks continue to be treated to this very generation.

This writer was privileged to know a Jewish man who faced the same kind of dilemma which confronted Hank half a century earlier. Kivie Kaplan was born in Russia, came to America as a boy, and grew up to become a wealthy and successful shoe manufacturer in Boston. One day he was driving in his chauffeured limousine in Miami Beach. He saw a sign that read, "No dogs, kikes, or niggers."

That sign, insulting to Jews and blacks, changed his life. Kivie was shocked into action and decided then and there to devote his life to combating hatred of all kinds. He found his way to the National Association for the Advancement of Colored People (NAACP), a black civil rights organization, and he placed his wealth and his boundless energy at its disposal. He developed a fund-raising effort for the NAACP, crisscrossed the country to organize for civil rights, risked his life in the Deep South, and became the national president of the NAACP as well as the vice-chairman of the Commission on Social Action of Reform Judaism. To Kivie Kaplan, being Jewish meant a lifetime battle for social justice and equal rights for all—Jews, blacks, Hispanics, any group. His life symbolized the ideal of black-Jewish solidarity.

Jews despise racism because of our religion and because of our history. In modern Israel, many of our fellow Jews—from India, Morocco, Yemen, Ethiopia—are dark-skinned. We Jews are a multiracial people. To despise somebody for having a different skin color is to despise the God who fashioned Adam out of the many colors of the clay of the earth so that no one in future generations could ever claim, "My color makes me superior to you."

Blood Sisters

When the Civil War broke out in 1861, as described in the last story, most American Jews were new immigrants from Germany, Hungary, and Austria. In America today, however, most Jews come from families who arrived in the United States *after* the Civil War. These families came from Eastern Europe, especially Russia and Poland, which they left chiefly to escape anti-Semitism.

The anti-Semitism of Eastern Europe was as violent as the anti-Semitism of the Spanish Inquisition in its day. Russian Jews were segregated and discriminated against; Jewish boys were made to serve in the Russian army for twenty-five years. Worst of all, the Jews had to face vicious anti-Jewish riots called "pogroms." These were organized by the government whenever the poor people of Russia began to grumble about their hard lives. By taking out their anger on the Jews, the poor people of Russia would forget about the *real* causes of their trouble. In this way the Russian rulers and wealthy landowners avoided having to face a revolution until 1917. Meanwhile the Jews suffered or fled.

During the years from 1881 to 1914, the pogroms became so bad that over one-third of the Jews of Eastern Europe left their homes. The great majority, about two million, emigrated to America. Here there was religious freedom, and here there were job opportunities, especially in the growing clothing business in New York.

Other Jews went to modern Western European countries where it seemed that anti-Semitism was not so bad. And some

Jews, though not very many, became Zionists and went as pioneers to Palestine, the ancient Jewish homeland.

Palestine had not been a Jewish-run country for about 1,900 years, since the year 70 when the Romans had destroyed the Second Temple in Jerusalem, but some Jews had remained in Palestine ever since, living as a minority among the Arabs for many, many generations. The Zionists, however, wanted more than simply to live in Palestine as a Jewish minority. They wanted to build the country into a prosperous Jewish homeland to which Jews from all over the world might return and not have to worry about anti-Semitism. This was the Zionist dream: to end anti-Semitism by giving Jews, once again, a country of their own.

The Zionists did some amazing things in Palestine. They transformed barren land and swamps into farms, and they became expert farmers. They made Hebrew, which for centuries had been used only as a language for prayer, into a language for everyday conversation. They built roads, factories, and even the brand new city of Tel Aviv. They improved life for everyone in Palestine, including the poor Arabs who lived there. Still, unrest and mistrust grew between the Jews and Arabs in Palestine.

One reason for the tension was that Palestine was not a free country. Until World War I (1914–1918), it was under the control of the Ottoman Empire (Turkey). In 1920, after World War I, Great Britain became the ruling power in Palestine. In order to build a Jewish homeland there, the Zionists had to bargain with the rulers of these foreign powers. As the Palestinian Arabs began to think about their own independence, they came to view the Zionists as an enemy. The Jews, thought the Arabs, were in Palestine to help the British keep control.

In fact, the British *did* want to keep control of Palestine. They knew that, if Palestine became independent, other British colonies such as India might demand their independence, too. The British therefore helped create bad feelings between Arabs and Jews. By making them into enemies, the British could hide the fact that the real problem in Palestine was Great Britain itself.

Another cause for difficulty in Palestine was that the Arab leaders, mostly wealthy landowners, were afraid that the Jews would inspire the Arab peasants to demand a better life for themselves. The Jews, after all, were bringing modern industry, health care, machinery, and new ideas to the country. When the peasants saw this, would they continue to tolerate their own poverty and backward way of life? The Arab rulers had good reason, therefore, to turn the peasants' anger against the Jews—just as the Russian rulers had turned the Russian peasants' anger against the Jews.

Still another part of the problem in Palestine was that, instead of building bonds of friendship, the Zionists separated themselves from the Arabs. The Zionists saw Palestine as a place where Jews, by their own hard work, could build their national identity and become independent of all other peoples. They didn't want to hire Arab workers, therefore, or live in Arab villages. They tended to treat Palestine as if no one else lived there, and the Arabs deeply resented this.

Finally, there was the danger of religious conflict between the Jews and the Arabs. Some Arabs were Christian; most were Moslems, believers in Islam. Although Jews and Arabs had lived together in peace for centuries, their religious differences *could* become an excuse to provoke violence.

It is important to remember that many Jews around the world thought Zionism was a crazy idea—beautiful, perhaps, but mad. No one knew that in just a few years the Holocaust would suddenly make the Jewish people desperate for a homeland. Many American and European Jews believed they were successfully blending in ("assimilating") with the cultures of the countries in which they lived. Zionism, these Jews feared, would call too much attention to the fact that they were Jewish. Other Jews believed that only revolutions in the countries where Jews lived would put an end to anti-Semitism. Some Orthodox Jews were against Zionism for being essentially a secular, not a religious, movement.

Most of these disagreements were temporarily put aside in 1929, when the Jewish Agency was established. This was an international Jewish organization of Zionists and non-Zionists, dedicated to helping build Jewish life in Palestine. But the Arab leadership in Palestine looked upon the Jewish Agency with great fear —a fear made worse by their anti-Semitic beliefs about Jewish greed and power. These Arab leaders decided, therefore, to put an end to Zionism once and for all. In 1929, the Jews of Palestine, most of whom had come to escape the pogroms of Eastern Europe, faced another pogrom—an Arab pogrom, right there in the Holy Land. Almost two hundred Jews were killed in days of Arab rioting, including over seventy Jews in the ancient town of Hebron. Of these victims, many were not even Zionists but simply religious Jews—some Palestinians, some foreigners—who were studying at the great Lithuanian yeshivah of Slobodka there in Hebron.

At the time of the pogrom in late August, 1929, there were about 150,000 Jews and 750,000 Arabs living in Palestine. This story tells of the friendship between a Jewish girl and an Arab girl, both twelve years old. They are "blood sisters," in love with each other and with their land. But a river of blood also runs between them and keeps them apart. Their story is the story of the Jews and the Arabs in Palestine—a story that has not yet reached a happy ending today in modern Israel.

Hebron, Palestine: 1929

Five miles from Raymonda Khalidi's village was Zehava Bergelson's Jewish cooperative. It took over two hours for Raymonda to make that walk. Yet she hadn't been in Zehava's house for ten minutes before Zehava's mother seemed ready to throw her out.

"Jewish labor brings Jewish liberation," Mrs. Bergelson lectured Zehava, without even asking to be introduced to her friend. "If we let the Arabs do the work for us, we learn nothing and earn nothing. . . ."

"Momma," Zehava interrupted, "this is Raymonda Khalidi, and she's a friend. She's not working *for* me, she's working *with* me. We're going to make maps together. I'm teaching her how."

"Maps-shmaps! The land doesn't need its portrait drawn! It

needs sweat," said Mrs. Bergelson, squinting at the Arab girl. "Where is she from, anyway?"

"The other side of Hebron," Zehava said. "I made her a map to show her how to get here."

"You made her what?"

"A map! Where's the map I made you, Rayzl?" She liked to make Raymonda's name sound Jewish. "I want to show my mom."

Raymonda shook her head. "I . . . I do not have it."

"Then how'd you get here?"

"I walked."

Zehava laughed. "See?" she said to her mother. "She knows Palestine like nobody else! We're going to make fantastic maps."

Mrs. Bergelson stared at Raymonda with deep suspicion. Raymonda, although she knew it was impolite, stared right back. She couldn't get over how filthy the woman's hands and face were.

"She speaks Hebrew, I see," Mrs. Bergelson said to her daughter.

"Uh-huh," Zehava said enthusiastically. "And English. And she's teaching me Arabic. Raymonda's real smart, Mom, and she never even went to school."

"Zehava, *hit zich vi fun a feier!*" (Be careful that you don't get burned!) *"Farshtayst?"* (Understand?) Mrs. Bergelson was speaking in Yiddish for the first time since they had come to Palestine —the first time in seven years!—just so Raymonda would not understand. "And now, tell her to go home—in any language you like." Mrs. Bergelson switched back into Hebrew. "Bad enough that the Arabs make slaves of their women and girls. We will not do the same."

"Momma! She's not . . ."

"Zehava! *Genug!"* (Enough!) Mrs. Bergelson threw a dirty rag over her shoulder and went into the yard to pump water.

"God damn it!" groaned Zehava, stamping her foot.

Raymonda's eyes grew wide as she heard this curse. "Please, Zehava, do not curse God for my sake."

"What? Oh, that's just an expression," Zehava said, and again she whined, "God damn it!"

Then she walked Raymonda back to the road. "My mom's got these crazy ideas about work. . . ."

"I can see this," Raymonda said, "from her hands. Excuse me for saying this, but never have I seen such dirty hands on a woman."

Zehava laughed and explained: "My dad was a truck mechanic. He died from malaria just a year after we came here from Poland."

Raymonda blessed Mr. Bergelson's memory in Arabic. "And your mother did not remarry?"

"Nah. She married Poppa's tools instead. My mom's the best mechanic on our cooperative. I bet you there's nothing in Palestine that she can't fix. You see, Rayzl . . ." Zehava hooked arms with the Arab girl. "For a Jew in Palestine to have clean hands is a shame. We want to work. We weren't allowed to work the land in Poland."

Raymonda nodded thoughtfully. "I understand. But in this we are very different. For an Arab woman to have clean hands—that is her great pride. It shows that her work—hundreds of years of work on the land—is finished, for the day at least." Raymonda stopped walking and turned to face her friend. "Perhaps that is why my grandfather says that the Jews are all over, taking over, everywhere. You work and you work without stop, like little birds that have been set free from a cage and must build their nests for the first time. While we . . ." Raymonda stretched her arms out like wings. "We float, like great, big birds that sail in the air and watch over the land." Then she reached to touch Zehava's thick, loose hair. "And we see your bright feathers, and we remember that you are here." And she touched her own hair, braided and hidden beneath a scarf. "And you see only our drab feathers— you don't even notice us."

"You don't even notice an Arab," Zehava suddenly remembered hearing someone in her town say, "until his knife is in your back." "Uch," she thought, "what a horrible thing to say! Where did I hear that?"

Raymonda kissed her cheek. "But I think both kinds of birds are good. Both birds belong in Palestine, praised be Allah."

Zehava smiled nervously and looked away from Raymonda's piercing eyes.

"You are unhappy," Raymonda observed. "What is it?"

Zehava quickly shook her head, "I'm just sorry that you have to go," she said. "I'm mad at my mother. I don't understand her. And we didn't even get to look at any of my big maps."

Raymonda smiled at her. "No, I did not learn more about maps today. But we learned about each other's hands, a little—and they are a kind of map, don't you think?"

Zehava sighed. "And now you've got to walk the whole way home! Hey, why don't you take my bicycle, Rayzl?"

Raymonda giggled at the idea and, with a wave of her hand, began her five-mile trek.

Zehava stalked back to her house in an angry mood. She found her mother still by the water pump, wiping her hands dry while three chickens circled and clucked at her feet.

"Why did you do that?" Zehava demanded to know. "Why did you chase her away?"

Mrs. Bergelson shook her finger in Zehava's face. "No, no; *I* will ask the questions. Who is this girl? Who is her father?"

"Their name is Khalidi. Raymonda's grandfather manages the vineyards in their town—the landlord is in Syria."

"I see."

"You see what?" Zehava said. "Why are you . . . ?"

"Sha!"

Rarely did Mrs. Bergelson raise her voice or act with such authority towards her daughter as this morning. Since Mr. Bergelson's death, they had been more like sisters, or pals, sharing many decisions as they worked together to build their home. But today Zehava could see that her mother meant business.

"And this map that you gave her, what did it show?"

"Who knows?" Zehava said sullenly.

"Who should know if not you?" her mother hollered. "Tell me, Zehava, or so help me God . . ."

"Okay! Okay, let me think. There was our house—and a few other houses as landmarks. I had to draw a lot of detail, you know, since she can't read whatever I wrote . . . and there was the road —and the storehouse—the machine shop. . . ."

"Ach!" Mrs. Bergelson slapped her leg in frustration. The chickens at her feet jumped in fright.

The machine shop! Now Zehava remembered. It was there, where her mother worked all day, that Zehava had heard the comment about Arabs stabbing you in the back. It had come from a Jew, a tall, young stranger who had driven a small truck and unloaded wooden crates into the shop. Zehava, once she saw that there was no romantic interest between her mother and the driver (though they spoke quietly, almost in whispers), had snuck away to avoid the heavy lifting.

"And when," Mrs. Bergelson continued the questioning, "did you give her the map?"

"The last time I saw her," Zehava replied, "which was Wednesday . . . no, Tuesday. We meet on Tuesdays, always in the same place in Hebron. She comes with her father to the mosque. I think," she added with a giggle, "he's showing her off to find her a husband!"

"Since when?"

"What do you mean?"

"Since when have you been meeting? Come on, Zehava, it's like pulling teeth with you. I want to know *everything!*"

They had first met in Hebron, one of the oldest towns in Palestine. The Arabs call it Khalil al-Rahman, the Beloved of the Merciful. Zehava had ridden her bicycle there (her mother had helped her make the bike out of spare parts the month before). She was carrying a notebook full of her homemade maps and taking notes for a new one, a map of the holy places in Hebron.

She came to Kharam, a Moslem mosque below which lies the

cave of Machpelah. Here Abraham and Sarah, Isaac and Rebecca, and Jacob and Leah are supposed to be buried. Raymonda was sitting outside the walled area while her father prayed inside the mosque. She was having her palm read by an old Druse woman. Zehava noticed this and was fascinated. She came closer to watch —and then she saw the snake!

It was a poisonous adder, small but deadly, and it was about to bite the Arab girl. Zehava dropped her books and drew the knife that her father had given her, which she always wore on her belt. The old fortune-teller saw her coming and screamed, thinking that the girl was crazy and dangerous. Raymonda saw what was happening by looking where Zehava was looking and managed to jerk her leg away just as the snake lunged. In a second, Zehava had her foot planted against the back of the snake's head; just as fast, her knife was red with blood.

Killing the snake made her dizzy. The summer heat suddenly felt overwhelming. She staggered and dropped her knife, nearly fainting. Raymonda rushed to her side, shooed away the crowd that had begun to gather, and brought Zehava to a shady spot, meanwhile thanking her, in Arabic, for being so brave.

For the first fifteen minutes of their friendship, Raymonda spoke only in Arabic, which Zehava hardly understood. Still they managed to have a conversation, mostly in sign language, about simple things. Zehava asked for water. Raymonda asked to see her knife. Then Zehava realized: "All my things!" she cried in Hebrew while moving her hands around frantically. "They're on the ground over by the fortune-teller. Someone will steal them!"

"I will get them for you," said Raymonda—in perfect Hebrew.

"So she tried to trick you," Mrs. Bergelson said as she listened carefully to her daughter's story.

"It wasn't a trick," Zehava insisted. "She explained it to me. She said that Jews expect Arabs to speak Hebrew, right? Even though most of us don't know Arabic. This way we were equal. Both of us had to work at the conversation."

Mrs. Bergelson frowned. "She's a real nationalist, I see."

Zehava shrugged. "So? Aren't we Jewish nationalists?"

"Go on, go on," Mrs. Bergelson said. "Tell me the rest."

"Now," Raymonda said with a handsome smile, "what are all these papers of yours?"

Zehava, relieved that nothing had been stolen, eagerly showed her work. Her book was full of the pencil drawings for larger maps that she made at home. Soon she realized that Raymonda did not know how to read and had never before looked closeup at maps. Zehava went on to explain all about the different kinds of maps—topographical, nautical, relief, physical—and what they were used for—navigation, land surveying, travel, political boundaries. . . .

Raymonda listened in silence. When Zehava was finished with her little lecture, Raymonda asked, "And why do you make these maps?"

"But I just told you!" Zehava said. "Didn't you understand?"

"Yes, I understand. But why do *you* make them?"

Zehava had never really asked herself that question; she was more of a doer than a thinker. Both her father and she had always shared an interest in art, although her mother had always discouraged that interest. "Better one farmer than ten artists," Mrs. Bergelson would say. "Artists do not make deserts bloom." "Oh, Momma," Zehava would think when she heard that, "how wrong you are!" Well, then, perhaps this mapmaking was simply a way to put her creative talent to useful work; a way to be an artist and a Zionist all at once; a way, also, to feel close to her father's memory. She began to express these thoughts, which were new and exciting to her.

But Raymonda spoke first. "I know that the British make these maps to conquer our land. My grandfather says they want to divide the Arab nation into many little parts. He says this of the Jews, too. Is it true?"

Zehava spoke bluntly: "Your grandfather sounds like he's anti-Jewish."

Raymonda arched her eyebrows. "So he is wrong about the Zionists?"

To be honest, Zehava could not answer this simply. There were some Zionists, yes, who wanted to rule over the whole land. There were others who wanted a government that would be both Jewish and Arab. Still others were satisfied to build Palestine into a spiritual center for Jews, with no Jewish government. In fact, most Zionists were simply too busy to give much thought to the Arabs. . . .

"Of course," Raymonda said, "it is not an easy question. There are good and bad in all peoples, and in each person." Then she took hold of Zehava's hand. Zehava was startled and almost pulled away, but Raymonda held her hand firmly. "Sh. I would not hurt you, ever. The snake's blood is fresh on your hands. We are blood sisters, you and I." She began to trace the lines of Zehava's palm, as the old Druse woman had done for her. "I do not know how to read palms," Raymonda admitted. "But I know that some come to the palm reader to know the future so they can get rich. Others want their palms read so they can find the path for their souls to follow, so their souls should not have to wander. So . . ." She folded Zehava's fingers into a fist and stared into her eyes. "Which are you?"

Zehava stared back at the mysterious Arab girl and, for the first time since her father had died, she thought: "What am I doing here, in this strange land?"

Mrs. Bergelson covered her ears, tugged her hair, and nearly screamed. "I can't stand to hear any more! I can't believe my daughter is so stupid! This Arab girl fills your ears with hocus-pocus and propaganda—and then you draw maps to show her grandfather how to come with his peasants to kill us!"

"What?" cried Zehava. "Are you crazy? No! Raymonda is my friend! She is! She wants to help me make maps! She'll help me understand Palestine!"

Mrs. Bergelson spat on the ground. "Understand it, yes. Understand it with a nice, long blade in your guts! My God, Zehava, how can you be so naive?"

"I'm not! You don't know her! You don't know what you're talking about!"

"I don't have to know her! If she's not a deliberate spy, then she's being used as one. You come with me!" Mrs. Bergelson grabbed Zehava by the arm.

"Where are we going?"

"Come! We're going to the machine shop—where I slave a whole day while you busy yourself with maps! I'm going to show you what's happening in the real world, Zehava—the *real* Palestine!"

The machine shop was a filthy place, strewn with metal and oil, tools and dirty rags. But Mrs. Bergelson knew exactly what she was looking for amid the junk. She pulled back an oily piece of canvas, and Zehava recognized what was underneath: the crates that the stranger, the one who didn't like Arabs, had unloaded from his truck.

"What are they?" Zehava said in a low voice.

"Rifles," said her mother. "Guns. Ammunition. All illegal. If the British knew we had these, we'd be arrested. But we have them and we'll keep them and we'll use them if we must. When the Arabs come, we're going to defend ourselves. We haven't worked and died on this land for all these years in order to be driven away by pogromists!"

"Pogroms? Oh, Momma!" Zehava said, almost laughing. "Where do you think we are, in Poland?"

Mrs. Bergelson lifted her hand to slap Zehava's face. Zehava backed away in shock. "You little brat!" her mother yelled. "Why don't you read newspapers? Why don't you pay attention to what's going on around you? I should never have made you that bicycle, Zehava—never! I thought it would interest you in machinery, in mechanics, in useful work. Instead it gets you interested in Arab lies. Now, you listen to me," she went on. "The Grand Mufti of Jerusalem—that no-good, anti-Semitic bastard of an Arab leader!—he's been making threats against our people.

Not in his own words, oh, no! He's too smart for that! He wants the British and the rest of the world to think of him as a soft-spoken, peace-loving leader. But why is it, then, that all of his followers are spreading lies about us? The sheikhs, the mullahs, the landowners—people like your darling friend's grandfather!—all of them are smearing the land of Palestine with their anti-Jewish garbage. One says we are planning to bomb the Mosque of Omar in Jerusalem. Another says that we're arranging through the Jewish Agency to buy all of Palestine from the British for some ungodly sum of money. Oh, yes!" Mrs. Bergelson waved her hands furiously. "So much money we have! The Jews are filthy rich! That's why we came to this desert of a country to live! That's why we raise chickens for food! That's why I slave my life away with my hands in grease! That's why I could not save my husband from malaria but had to watch him die—because I'm so rich!"

She was out of her mind with anger. Zehava wanted only to calm her mother, to quiet her down and make her feel better. But as soon as Zehava opened her mouth to speak, Mrs. Bergelson jumped down her throat. "And with all of this, *you* choose to take an Arab for a girl friend! You let her make you doubt everything that your father and I ever taught you. You let her make you feel that you don't belong in Palestine. And then you invite her into our house so she can see where we sleep and come back with an axe to chop our heads off! No, Zehava! We *do* belong in Palestine, and we're going to fight! We have to fight! The British won't help us, you see. They won't raise a finger to protect us because they're afraid that, if they do, they'll have an Arab revolt on their hands. Well, maybe that's what they deserve! But the Arab revolution is not going to wave a flag stained with Jewish blood! Arab national-ism will not be built upon the bodies of Jews! No! I say no! We'll never again be a scapegoat! Either the Arabs will learn to live with us in Palestine—or they'll die with us in Palestine!"

With this curse, Mrs. Bergelson picked up a crowbar. "And now," she said, prying open one of the crates, "you're going to learn how to clean and oil a rifle, Zehava. You and I are going to work until you drop. You won't have time or energy left for your fantasy world of maps and sweet Arab girls. Today you are a woman, Zehava! *Mazal tov!* Say goodbye to your childhood!"

They worked like slaves, without stopping to eat, until well after dark. Zehava, filthy and exhausted, fell into bed with her clothes on, but could not sleep. Worse than any of her mother's news, worse than any nightmares of violence or murder or anti-Semitism, was the thought that Raymonda could not be trusted. It was enough to drive Zehava crazy.

True, they were afraid of each other. Zehava knew this. Her uncovered head, her hair streaming freely; her ability to go wherever she pleased, whenever she pleased; her knife, and her courage, and her physical strength; her education, her ability to read and know about the world beyond Palestine; her mother who needed no husband, who worked like a man with machinery and tools—all of this, Zehava knew, was frightening to Raymonda. It made the Arab girl realize how the Moslem tradition was a tight trap for a girl her age. It made her question her own culture.

And Raymonda's ability to speak three languages; her deep knowledge of the land, as if it were all mapped out in her mind; her lovely, searching eyes, which could see into Zehava's heart and know her secrets; her maturity and the mystery that lay behind her shy Moslem appearance—all of this was frightening to Zehava. It made her see how new she was to Palestine—still almost a visitor!—and how fragile a hold the Jewish people had on their homeland.

Yes, they frightened each other by being different—but only when they were apart. Together the differences blended creatively, like sunshine and air, like water and soil, and they became blood sisters again. Oh, why had her mother not listened to the rest of Zehava's story?

Four times the girls had met in Hebron, at the spot where the snake had been killed. Usually Raymonda was with her father, waiting for his prayers to be done; once she had come alone. She and Zehava would walk around the town, and talk about the world, and share their feelings, creating, out of their friendship, a living map of Palestine—a Palestine where their peoples could live together and recognize each other's beauty and wisdom. Could it be that such a Palestine existed only on paper? Only when they looked into each other's eyes? Only while the adults prayed, or worked, or slept?

"My God," thought Zehava, almost as if in prayer herself, "does growing up mean that all love turns to hatred? Is that what it means? Then I don't want to grow up at all!"

The night deepened, and the full moon shined through her window. Zehava slept only for short moments, each time jerking awake from bad dreams. Finally she sat up, wide awake. She couldn't sleep—she would never sleep again if she did not find out the truth about her friendship! She strapped on her sandals, grabbed her knife, and covered her head in Arab fashion. She studied her book of maps, reminding herself of all the trips she'd taken, on foot and on bicycle, to create them. If she could just find her way from Hebron to Raymonda's village, she was sure she could find Raymonda's house. "It's the biggest in our village," Raymonda had said. "And I have my own room, next to the garden, now that my sisters are married. . . ."

Zehava sneaked out of her house. Because of all the rumors about anti-Semitism among the Arabs, there would be someone from the collective on guard duty, probably near the machine shop. Zehava picked up her bicycle and walked it around the back of her house, across an open field, and up to the road. No one noticed; no one shouted for her to stop. The land was as still as a drawing on a map.

Now she mounted her bicycle and rode into the night. Her only light was the moon, but it was full and high in the clear sky, bathing the hills with a spooky, creamy light. She knew her way to Hebron with ease, and it took her only half an hour to weave her way across the quiet, sleeping town. But on the western side of Hebron were several dusty roads leading to several Arab villages. The name Khalidi might have been familiar to a local Arab since Raymonda's grandfather was a fairly powerful man in the area, with many peasants working for him. But there was no one around to ask. Besides, Zehava would have been afraid to speak to anyone at this hour of the night.

"I think it's this way. . . ." There was no time for doubt; she had to make up her mind which way to go. She had to move quickly, as with the snake. Zehava took out her knife and tossed it in the air. Whichever way its blade pointed when it fell . . .

Good! Just as she thought . . .

It was all like a dream; even more so when Raymonda appeared at her window in a nightgown and whispered, "Praised be Allah! I was just dreaming about you!"

"And I dreamed about you," Zehava said softly. "But they were terrible dreams. Come outside."

"I should not," Raymonda said. "I am confined."

A shiver went down Zehava's spine. "What do you mean, 'confined'?"

"It . . . it happened to me today as I walked home from your village. I . . . I became a woman. I have the woman's curse, for the first time."

"Oh, my God!" Zehava said, then cupped her mouth to hush her own voice. "You got your period! *Mazal tov!*"

Then Zehava remembered that her mother had said the same —"*Mazal tov!*"—while screaming at her to grow up. Perhaps this was only Raymonda's trickery again. Perhaps her grandfather had told her to stay indoors, out of harm's way, while the men went forward to slaughter Jews. If she grabbed Raymonda's hand and forced her to come out through the window, Raymonda would scream. . . .

"And you?" Raymonda said. "You are still a girl?"

Zehava spoke in a dull voice. "I haven't gotten mine yet."

"Well, it is not so bad," Raymonda said innocently. "Very little blood. But for me—oh, dear, for me it will mean great change. I cannot go where I want—I cannot meet you in Hebron, not even with my father. He will not bring me places any more. And soon I will be married—when a suitable husband is found. I don't even want this. . . ."

Zehava was ready to cry. There was so much she wanted to say to Raymonda, so much to share. But every word of love was tied down by suspicion, every word. . . .

"What is it, Zehava? Your bad dreams? Why did you have bad dreams?"

Zehava forced herself to be strong. "Give me your hand," she commanded with a sniffle.

Raymonda obeyed. She held her hand out the window, palm up.

"You said we were blood sisters," Zehava said.

"Yes, we are. And we always will be. I will tell my husband, too."

"We are blood sisters," Zehava repeated. "And this means we have never lied to each other."

"Never."

"It means that we would never hurt each other on purpose."

"Never."

"It means that there is room in Palestine for both of us."

"Always, Zehava. Always."

Zehava drew her knife. "You swear all of this to me and to God?"

"Yes," agreed Raymonda.

"Then this will be our contract."

Raymonda let out a little cry as Zehava slashed the tip of her middle finger. Then Zehava cut her own and pressed their bleeding fingers together. "Oh, Raymonda," she said, "I love you. You are the best thing I have found in Palestine. You are my family. And I need to prove that to my mother. She's suspicious, Raymonda. She thinks that your grandfather—oh, it doesn't matter. Just get me the map, now. The map that I drew for you. My mother is scared for anyone but me to have it."

"But, Zehava! I do not have it! My grandfather, he took it from me and said he would add to your Hebrew names all of the Arabic names—then it would be a truly Palestinian map! He has not yet given it back, Zehava. Not yet, but . . ."

Commentary

This touching story of the love between a Jewish girl and an Arab girl took place in Palestine in the 1920s, a generation before the modern State of Israel was established. Could such a "blood friendship" have developed in those days? Yes. Could such a friendship occur today? Very, very unlikely. And in that difference lies much of the heartbreaking tragedy of Arab-Jewish conflict in the Middle East.

Although in their secret hearts Raymonda and Zehava were afraid of each other, the whispering gap of suspicion between them was bridged by their love. The sad fact is that, in the decades since, the fears of their families came true and created a deep chasm of hatred, filled with blood.

In the 1929 Arab pogrom in Hebron, incited by the Grand Mufti, Jews were killed, not as Zionists, but as Jews, some of them from families who had lived in Palestine for generations. Overnight the optimists on both sides who dreamed of a land shared by Jews and Arabs were pushed aside. Hearts hardened in both communities. Both sides armed themselves against the other. The vision of a shared destiny was shattered.

When the United Nations voted on November 29, 1947, to divide Palestine into two states, one Jewish and one Arab, the Jews accepted the terms of the partition although the Jewish state would be only half the area of Palestine. The Arab world furiously rejected the U.N. action and vowed to strangle the infant Jewish state in its crib. In the 1948 War of Independence, Israelis had to fight for their lives against Arabs seeking to "drown them in the sea." Israel won this war as it has won all the other Arab-Israel wars since. But distrust and resentment between Jews and Arabs have become so intense that even *within* the State of Israel relations between them are explosive.

With few exceptions, Arab Israelis are not permitted to serve in the Israeli army. Many feel they do not have the full rights of first-class citizenship, although Israeli Arabs do have the right to vote and to sit in the Knesset (Israel's parliament). Few Jews and

Arabs in Israel share personal friendships; most still hold the same negative, stereotypic beliefs about each other that were held by Raymonda's and Zehava's families. Israeli Jews regard Arabs as dirty, lazy, violent, corrupt, pro-PLO, and anti-Jewish. Israeli Arabs regard Jews as racist, aggressive, coarse, and exploitative.

The dream of many of the founders of Zionism was a Jewish state in which Arabs and Jews would build a harmonious and peaceful covenant together. The bitter reality is that historic events have actually deepened the Arab-Jewish rift. The emergence of the PLO and other Arab terrorist groups; the continued occupation by Israel of the largely Arab West Bank and Gaza; the growth of a Jewish terrorist group that believes Arabs should be driven from the West Bank so that the land will be in Jewish hands; the development of extremist, fundamentalist Arab groups who believe in a holy war against the Jewish "infidels"—all of this still frustrates the youthful dreams of Zehava and Raymonda.

In November, 1977, when President Anwar Sadat of Egypt electrified the world by going to Jerusalem to make peace with Israel, an opportunity to heal the troubled Middle East presented itself. The idealism of the Jewish people was deeply stirred. Egyptian flags fluttered throughout Israel. Hope flowered. Could Israel and Egypt, like Zehava and Raymonda, make an oath of peace in a region of the world drenched with hate?

Although a peace treaty was signed in March, 1979, it has produced a cold peace. Sadly, it has, as yet, not inspired any other Arab nations to sit down and negotiate with Israel. Instead, Sadat the peacemaker was assassinated by Moslem extremists in 1981, just as other Arab leaders who have openly sought peace with Israel have been murdered in the past.

Is the tender story of these two girls merely a quaint fantasy of what might have been? Perhaps not. There are Arabs and Jews who want desperately to coexist in mutual respect and friendship, and who have organized dialogues across the great divide between their peoples. For example, an organization called Interns for Peace trains young Jews in Arabic language and culture and sends them into Israeli Arab villages to promote integration and friendship. The higher the walls of hatred, the more necessary it is to find such passageways for Palestinian Arabs and Jews to discover what they have in common and learn to live together.

In fact, there are elements that make Israeli Arabs and Jews similar. Both are well-educated, the Palestinians being the best-educated segment of the Arab world. Both are enterprising and industrious peoples. Both have experienced the pain of home-lessness. Both wish to preserve their own cultures. Both, in the end, cannot survive without learning to live with the other.

Cultural differences do not have to divide people; they can unite people, making life richer and deeper. Ultimately there will be no future for Israel if Jews and Arabs cannot learn to respect one another. Raymonda and Zehava were not as naive as their families thought. True, maps can be used for fanatical violence, but they can also be used to point the way to people's hearts and examine how deeply similar are their hopes and needs.

Did God Create the Nazis?

The Holocaust—the murder of six million Jews by the German Nazis from 1939 to 1945—is the most tragically influential event in modern Jewish history. Over one-third of the Jews of the world—including 1.5 million children—were slaughtered for no reason other than being Jewish. Though we, as a people, were strong enough to survive such vicious anti-Semitism, Jewish life was nevertheless permanently changed by the Holocaust. Where we live, what languages we speak, how we view the world—all of this was changed by the Nazis.

For many religious Jews, the Holocaust presented a troubling question: Why did God permit the murder of so many Jews? Some could find no answer and lost their faith; others answered that the evil Nazis were doing "God's will," delivering God's punishment for some unknown sins committed by the Jewish people.

Many Jews, however, denied that God had any role in the destruction. The Holocaust, they said, was a human crime that could be stopped—or at least resisted. These Jews, religious and non-believing, with a variety of political views, fought the Nazis in the ghettos and concentration camps throughout Europe. Sometimes the fight was spiritual, as in helping a fellow human being survive in a death camp, keeping up Jewish customs under the worst conditions, or maintaining pride and dignity in the face of humiliation. Other times, Jews were able to fight militarily, although in these uprisings they were alone, outnumbered and with only primitive weapons. Still, the Jewish revolts against the

Nazis signaled to the world that the Jews were a proud, fighting people.

The most famous revolt of the Holocaust was the Warsaw Ghetto Uprising, which lasted from April 19–May 16, 1943. The uprising was led by Zionists, Communists, and Bundists, most of them young men and women, all Jews, all working together.

Their cause was hopeless. The Jews had few guns and little ammunition; the Nazis had tanks, flamethrowers, machine guns, and airplanes. The Jews were starved and sick; the Nazis were well-fed and had a large supply of fresh soldiers to send against the Jewish fighters. Yet the Jews fought on bravely, taking many Nazi lives, until finally the Germans burned the ghetto to the ground.

Warsaw, the capital of Poland, had been the center of Polish Jewish life before the Nazis invaded in 1939. Almost 400,000 Jews had lived in Warsaw, out of more than 3,000,000 Jews throughout Poland. By the time of the ghetto uprising, however, the Jewish population of Warsaw was no more than 70,000. From October 2, 1940, the Jews in Warsaw had been forced by the Nazis to live in a small area, divided from the rest of the city by a wall. In this ghetto, starvation and disease took thousands of lives. Thousands of others were shipped to such Nazi concentration camps as Auschwitz, the death camp in Poland where about 1,500,000 Jews perished, and especially to Treblinka where, from 1942, 200,000–300,000 Jews from Warsaw were sent for extermination.

The Jews who still lived in the Warsaw Ghetto in 1943 were deeply divided among themselves. Some wanted to cooperate with the Nazis, hoping that cooperation would mean survival. Others believed that the Holocaust was "God's will" and would not fight, even though they had nothing left to lose. Others were ready to fight until the end, to fight back and die with dignity rather than be shipped to an extermination camp.

This story, in the form of a diary, tells of an Orthodox boy in Warsaw in the days just before the uprising. He is torn between the religious beliefs of his father and the bravery and rebelliousness of the ghetto fighters. The boy has witnessed many terrible sights, including the death of his own mother, and he is now searching the ruins of the city to find the face of God, to ask God, "Why?" What he finds, instead, as we shall see, are the faces of the ghetto fighters, proud and grim as they prepare to fight the monster of anti-Semitism for their final time.

Warsaw, Poland: 1943

February 10

I do believe that Momma's soul has entered heaven because today, for the first time since she died, I can remember her as she used to look, strong, healthy, happy, and big. Just yesterday I could only imagine her as she looked in the end, so shriveled and yellow and old that I could hardly stand to think of her. It felt as if her soul were flying around and around this dark little room like a bat, afraid to leave me, afraid to leave Poppa, unable to rest. But now I do believe her rest has begun, and my memory of her has become beautiful again. This morning I woke up thinking of the sounds her pots and pans used to make. I could almost smell bread baking, and I could imagine her kneading the dough with her fat, jiggling arms.

I have dreams about food all the time, now, and yet I don't feel hungry anymore. I think my stomach has shrunk like a prune. But I must find some food, for Poppa and for me. Dr. Gluckman, who every Friday has visited with a bag of food, has not been here for two weeks. I'm afraid that he, too, must be dead, for he would never forget Poppa, who was his teacher in yeshivah.

I said this just now to Poppa, that I thought Dr. Gluckman is dead. Poppa didn't even hear me. That happens more and more every day—he doesn't hear, though he's sitting right there and never leaves this room. So much of him died with Momma! Every day his head gets heavier, his heart sinks deeper, and he sits at Dr. Gluckman's old desk, buried in his books. Maybe that's why I'm writing in this diary—to have someone who listens, to know that I'm still here.

This morning I remembered a feeling I once had as a very little boy when Momma took me on the trolley to go shopping. I looked at the passengers and suddenly I realized that each one of them had a whole world of ideas and thoughts, just like me. And each of them could see me only as I saw them, on the surface. Even Momma—even she was separate from me and could never really, really know me.

It was a terrible, scary feeling of being all alone.

That's when the feeling for G-d, the mitzvah of *bitachon*—trust in Hashem—truly entered my heart. G-d would be my friend. G-d would be the one who does come inside of me, who *is* me. Otherwise I would die of loneliness.

But we are dying and, in a certain way, it *is* from loneliness, for, if anyone in the world cared about us, the Nazis could not be doing what they're doing. So where is Hashem now? Are we not His chosen people anymore? Maybe the faith that I thought I had when I was little was just a way of consoling myself, like sucking my thumb?

I wish I could talk about this to Poppa, but he's . . . I don't know what he is or where he is. He's not here. He's not even eating the few remaining bits of food that we have. He just prays, eats words. How can I ever say to him, "Poppa, I think that G-d is just make-believe"?

But I must find out for myself. Let Poppa read in peace, but I cannot believe that Hashem lives inside the Torah anymore. If Hashem is real, then He must be walking the streets of our ghetto. There are such times when G-d comes nearer to us—terrible times, like in the Torah when He at last hears the groaning of the people of Israel in Egypt. And then G-d comes to have a look, to select Moses, to save His chosen people. I do believe that we are living in that kind of time.

I have to go out. I haven't been outside of this room for almost a month, since Dr. Gluckman brought us here and warned us to stay off the streets because the Germans were again going to do a roundup. They're trying to empty out the ghetto by Passover,

he said. And now I'm sure that Dr. Gluckman himself is dead, or gone. The Nazis aren't letting anybody escape, I guess, not even members of the Jewish Council.

Still, I must go out. Early tomorrow, before morning prayers, I'll unlock that window in the back and sneak outside for a while. Nobody will see me, I'll make sure. And Poppa probably won't even notice. If he does, good! At least I'll know he's alive!

Oh, why, why, why do I keep having this feeling that Poppa is dying?

O Most High, we are down to our last crust of bread, and my soul is even hungrier than my stomach.

February 19

It has changed out there, a lot. The streets of the ghetto are empty. Everyone who's left is in hiding, like us. There aren't even as many dead bodies as there used to be. And there's nothing to buy on the street. I couldn't find any food, not a thing, until I met the old lady and all that craziness began to happen.

But wait, my diary, wait. Before food, I must tell you about the sky! Big and blue and wide and so magnificent! I tried to take it all in with my eyes, the color, the space, so I could carry it back to our little prison. Oh, blessed art Thou, Lord our G-d, Ruler of the universe who provides us with moments to remind us of Creation!

So I walked and walked, just to feel the air against my face. It's so different outside in the cold, when you're moving, than inside, where you sit and shiver. I even visited our old street, Wolynska, and stopped in front of the building where we used to live. All the glass has been knocked out of the windows so you can't tell who's living where or if anybody's living there at all. I watched my own bedroom window for a while—but what can you see through cardboard? Well, if someone is there, may Hashem place a guardrail around them so they can live a long life.

Then came the old woman out of the doorway of the building. O diary, from the way she looked at me, she must have thought I was crazy. There I was, strolling through hell with a smile on my face! I guess it was crazy, even stupid. Do I really believe that Hashem is going to show me a sign of some kind the way He did for Moses in the wilderness, just because I go around making blessings over everything I see? And yet the ghetto *is* a wilderness —and the thing that happened, wasn't it a kind of sign?

The woman called to me. "There aren't so many youngsters left in Warsaw, sonny," she said. "Don't go showing yourself off in broad daylight. It's just about this time that the Nazis like to get to work, too."

I answered her by saying that there aren't many old people left in the ghetto either.

"Well, then," the old lady said—she had a very nice voice—"we ought to stick together, the young and the old." And then she reached into her apron and brought out a piece of bread for me.

So that's when it happened, just as I went to her for the bread. I was saying the blessing for this bit of nourishment, and suddenly a man came running down the street. The old woman pulled me into her doorway with a yank. I peeked out and saw that the man, a Jew, was breathing like a tired horse and sweating even though there's snow on the ground and it's freezing cold. And then I saw why he was sweating: I heard a gunshot, and the man spun around and almost fell against the wall. Two men were chasing him, two Nazis with guns. I began to pray with all my might that they wouldn't find us in the doorway because they would shoot us, I was sure. But the wounded man kept coming in our direction, and the old lady told me to please shut up. I didn't know what to do.

There were more shots. Then all of a sudden a big explosion tore up the street and blew those Nazis to bits. It must have been a bomb or a grenade of some kind. I could feel the explosion like a hot wind against my face. I don't know where it came from— maybe even from a window in my old building, it was that close! It seemed to drop right out of the heavens.

Then the old lady pulled the wounded man into the doorway and cursed him for coming there, for leading the Nazis to Wolyn- ska Street. They knew each other, I could tell that from the way they talked. Maybe the man was her son—it could be. But I realized from what they were saying that they belonged to the underground, the Jewish Fighting Organization.

I have never before seen people who belong to the underground. I've heard about them, I've seen their newspapers once or twice, but never before did I stand next to them and talk with them. Such ordinary-looking people! From the way Poppa talks about the Jewish Fighting Organization, I expected them to look like horrible madmen. Poppa says that *they* are the sinners for whom G-d is now punishing all of us. Could this be true?

The old lady told me, "You'd better go now, sonny. There will be more of those Nazi swine here at any minute." I wondered where *she* would go, especially with her wounded son or friend, whatever he is. I even thought of inviting them to Dr. Gluckman's office. But I knew that Poppa would throw them out —or else they might shoot him and take whatever we have left. Who can you trust? So I ran as quickly as I could. I suddenly felt terribly afraid. Was I afraid of them, or was I afraid because I was leaving them?

I recited the blessing for deliverance from danger, and then I looked back just before I turned the corner onto Zamenhofa Street. The old woman was standing next to the bloody pieces of the German's bodies. Uch! She was taking their guns, their bullets, whatever she could find, like a cat picking clean the bones of a bird. It was a horrible sight, but I must confess, only to you, my diary, that it thrilled me to see an old Jewish woman standing, alive, next to the bodies of our tormentors. Am I bad to have such feelings? It was the first time since Momma died that I felt some hope for the future, some hope that this sight—the Nazis dead, the Jews alive—was a vision of the future. Yet we are not supposed to rejoice at the death of sinners. As it is written in the Talmud: When the angels wanted to sing at the sight of the Egyptians drowning in the Red Sea, Hashem silenced them, saying, "The work of My hands is drowning in the sea, and you desire to sing songs!" But can it be true that the Germans, too, are the creation of Hashem?

February 26

Wonderful news! Dr. Gluckman is alive! He came to see us yesterday. He had two cans of fish stuffed into his pockets, which Poppa
opened with a key. A feast! We even drank the oil in the cans. And
then Dr. Gluckman told us what had happened to him. The Nazis
had arrested him in a sweep on Mila Street, and, even though he's
a member of the Jewish Council, they were going to transport him
to Treblinka. Then a high Nazi official was wounded badly—
either by accident or by the underground, Dr. Gluckman is not
sure which—and the Nazis decided that they needed the doctor's
services again.

"I saved his life in Gestapo headquarters," Dr. Gluckman told
us. "It was a difficult operation. There were five pieces of shrap-
nel in his back. Both the Gestapo doctor and I worked all through
the night."

By saving the Nazi bigshot's life, Dr. Gluckman saved his own.
"But," I heard him say in a low voice to Poppa, "I feel unclean."

Poppa tried to make him feel better by quoting from Mishnah
Sanhedrin: "If one saves a single life, it is as if one has saved the
world." But Dr. Gluckman wondered if the Mishnaic teachings
apply to the Nazis. He sounded sick and worried—like a little boy.
"Are the lives of the very worst of the *goyim* sacred, Rabbi?"

Again Poppa recited from the Talmud, from Rabbi Hillel:
"Whatever is hateful to you, do not do it to others. That is the
whole Law." And Poppa also quoted the Rambam, about how
true strength is found by being patient, by living with unhappiness, the way Job did. And then he asked Dr. Gluckman: Who was
wiser, Bar Kochba, who fought with weapons against the Romans
in a war that led to Israel's destruction, or Ben Zakkai, who saved
Judaism by leaving Jerusalem before the Romans destroyed the
city?

But Dr. Gluckman asked Poppa exactly the question that I was
thinking: If Ben Zakkai was wiser, then why are we still in Warsaw?
Why haven't we left, the way Ben Zakkai left Jerusalem?

That made Poppa laugh. "And where should we go?" he said.
"All of Poland is now Jerusalem! The Nazis have control every-

where! There is nothing, nothing between here and Treblinka but death!"

Can you imagine how I felt when I heard this? O my diary, dear diary! I have gotten used to hearing grownups speak in hopeless words, but still it scares me. If they don't understand what is happening to us, if they have no hope, then what are we young people to think?

Is this really the end of days? If yes, then I have nothing to fear, for I will just die like everyone else. It doesn't matter if Dr. Gluckman saves a Nazi or saves himself—we will all die soon enough. I wonder if that's how the people in the Jewish Fighting Organization feel. That man in the street, and the old woman, do they believe that their guns will bring them life? Or do they know that they're going to die anyway, no matter what they do? And what about Poppa? Does he pray and study and fast in hope of redemption—or only to welcome in the Angel of Death?

I got up my courage and asked Poppa this question. It has never been easy to ask him questions; he always turns them around on you, and it becomes a test of your knowledge. "Poppa," I said, "do you believe as Ben Zakkai believed that we and our faith will outlive the Nazis? Or are you just saying Kaddish all the time for Momma, for my sisters, for everybody? Is there any hope, Poppa?"

I can't describe the look that came into my father's eyes. He looked angry at me and frightened of me at the same time. All he said was, "G-d moves in mysterious ways."

Then I said, "But . . ."

And he yelled, "There are no buts! It is the young Jews who say 'But, but' all the time—the Jews without faith, without beards, the Jewish Communists and Bundists and Zionists—*these* are the ones for whom Hashem is punishing all of Israel!" And he kept screaming and screaming at me until I ran and hid by face.

March 7

This morning I began to wonder how many Jews have died since the Nazis appeared? Thousands, maybe hundreds of thousands?

Millions? If we've been dying all over as quickly as we are dying in Warsaw, then yes, it is millions. But these are just numbers, thousands, millions. So I began thinking of all the Jewish names I know. Shmul, Mordecai, Leib, Yeshua, Yitzhak, Avrom, Asser, Beryl . . . Tsil, Leah, Feige, Hanna, Dvera, Buzie, Ruchel . . . I counted two hundred and forty-five, including every name I could think of from the Torah, and then finally I stopped. Two hundred and forty-five! It takes four times that to make a thousand. It takes four thousand times that to make a million! Four thousand Shmuls, four thousand Moishes, four thousand Chaikas . . .

March 18

Dr. Gluckman says we have to move. He says the Germans are telling him to give over any remaining children in the ghetto. If they ever find out that I'm living here in his own office, we'll all be shot.

How sorry I feel for this man when he comes to us! He has such a guilty look on his face, all because he is on the Jewish Council and must obey the Nazis' orders. He makes lists of people who are able to do labor, which means to live. If you're not on the list that Dr. Gluckman gives to the Germans, either you'd better hide or you're as good as dead. Dr. Gluckman always says to Poppa, "If I don't obey, it will be worse for everybody. This way at least I can protect *some* of our people." But then he also weeps and says things like, "I should strangle myself with my own hands! There is so much Jewish blood on these hands!"

Anyway, we must move. Dr. Gluckman is bringing us tomorrow evening to a place on Smocza Street. It is a bunker, a hiding place, he says. There are Jews there with food, with a radio, with enough things to keep us alive for months. Dr. Gluckman says we should not give up hope. The Nazis have taken a beating from the Russians, he says. Maybe Hitler will at last get what he deserves.

The thought of living through all of this seems awful to me. To have to live and grow up knowing that my mother was murdered, my sisters were murdered, all my friends were murdered, and I'm still alive—I think I'd rather die.

Oh, but if *I* feel this way, my diary, can you imagine how Poppa feels? I've been trying to figure out why he acts so angry with me, why he hardly ever talks unless Dr. Gluckman is here for a visit. Poppa used to be so proud of me. He used to call me his "little scholar," and he would tell me that I would grow up to be a miracle-working rabbi, a great, wise teacher. And yet I am the same person now that I was before the Nazis came and ruined our lives. I'm still a good Jew, and I try to be a good son.

They say that all wisdom is in the Torah. So today I studied the Akedah, the part where Abraham is told to sacrifice his son, Isaac. I thought about how Abraham must have felt when G-d gave him that order. He must have gotten very mad at Isaac even though Isaac hadn't done anything wrong. Because if Abraham didn't get mad at Isaac, he'd have to get mad at Hashem, and that would be a sin. Or else he'd have to get so mad at himself that he would die. He would explode from the anger inside and die. So instead he turned it against his son. I know I'm right, too, because of how Hashem had to call Abraham's name twice before he put down his knife and saw the ram caught in the bushes. Abraham was so angry at Isaac that he didn't hear G-d calling him.

And that's how Poppa feels about me. I've figured it out. He looks at me each day and feels how hopeless our future is. He feels how all his prayers and all his study are unable to save us. He knows that I will probably not even live to be bar mitzvah next year. So the only way that Poppa can keep himself from losing his love for G-d is by taking away his love for me.

So then I was thinking about the old woman from the underground and the way she looked at me—with love in her eyes, with excitement, just because I'm young and alive. I guess she doesn't believe in G-d. Or she believes you can hate the Nazis without hating Hashem because Hashem did not send the Nazis. And because she is able to curse the Nazis and throw grenades at them, she can smile at me.

So maybe Poppa is all wrong about the Nazis. He says that they are doing the work of Hashem, punishing our people for their sins. We should hate the sinful Jews, he says, not the Nazis. But maybe Hashem wants us to fight back. Maybe the fighters of the Jewish Fighting Organization are the righteous ones because they know that G-d is not to blame for our trouble. Maybe it is Poppa who does not understand the will of Hashem! "If I am not for myself," Rabbi Hillel taught us, "who will be for me?" Doesn't the underground obey these words better than Poppa?

I am glad to be leaving this place. It'll be good to live among other Jews, Jews who have hope. Sometimes with Poppa I feel like we're already dead.

But don't worry, diary, I won't abandon you. You are my heart, wherever I go.

March 19

A horrible thing has happened. Dr. Gluckman has killed himself.

It happened just a few hours ago, at about eight o'clock, which was when he was supposed to take us to Smocza Street. An envelope fell onto the floor of our room through the slot that the doctor uses to contact us. Poppa began to read it, and then suddenly we heard a shot in the main part of the house. We would have run there, but the door to this room is locked from the outside. Only Dr. Gluckman has the key. Our only way out of the room has been the window.

The note in the envelope came from the doctor. It said he could not bear to live any more. It said that the place where he was going to bring us is actually a hideout for the Jewish Fighting Organization, and Dr. Gluckman knew that Poppa would feel betrayed when we got there. But there is nowhere else to go in the ghetto. Either you go to Treblinka or you go to the underground. That's what the note says. And maybe by taking his own life, he would be protecting Poppa and me by letting us stay in the office. Yes, the Nazis will come looking for him, but when they find his body, they probably won't search further, G-d willing. Then all we have to do is feed ourselves.

I have been reading and rereading the note for hours. Poppa won't touch it. He acts like it's an unclean thing. This is how it ends:

Goodbye, dear teacher. You were all I had left in this world to make me feel like a human being, but it is not enough to keep me here. Please, do not feel responsible for this. It's just a matter of today or tomorrow or the next week—the Nazis have robbed my soul piece by piece, and I cannot bear to live longer. I know that you and the boy will think, "But just last night, he told us to have hope." Yet I realized afterwards that I do not want to survive this holocaust—there is too much blood on my hands, too much horror in my eyes. Perhaps by dying now, instead of waiting, I can help to preserve this sanctuary for you and help preserve your learnedness for Judaism. If that is so, I will be redeemed. Your loyal servant, Hyman Gluckman.

And now, dear diary, there is lots of noise on the street—gunshots, people yelling. It is much later in the night now, and I guess the Jewish Fighting Organization is doing its work. And that means that more Nazis will visit our neighborhood tonight. They will probably search all the houses and shoot anyone they find. Dr. Gluckman's death will not protect us, not in the slightest.

Poppa stands with his head against the door, crying and praying for the doctor. Somewhere beyond that door Dr. Gluckman's body is lying, and next to it must be the gun that he used. That's all I'm thinking of—his gun! How I wish I could get it and give it to the Jews who are battling for life on the streets of Warsaw!

O Most High! Why should we turn our guns on ourselves? If Dr. Gluckman wanted to die, why didn't he first shoot the biggest and worst Nazi he could find? Isn't it bad enough that we must be slaves to them, that we do whatever they say, work ourselves to death, get on board the trains, give whatever they ask for? Must we also do their dirty work and murder ourselves?

No! As it is written in the Torah: "Choose life!" Let the Nazis be the ones who deliver death to us. Our guns must not kill Jews!

I remember this midrash: When the people of Israel found themselves trapped between the waters of the Red Sea and the spears of the Egyptian army, and the Lord said to Moses, "Why do you cry out to me? Tell the Israelites to go forward," then one man, an ordinary Jew named Nachshon, took the first step into the water—and then the Red Sea split open!

Dear diary, I am leaving as soon as Poppa falls asleep. I am going out the window to the street, into the Red Sea, the Sea of Blood that is our ghetto. Watch over my father, O my heart, and try to preserve him. Preserve yourself, too, my diary, for future generations of Jews to read—if any of our people live to create such a future. But I, I am going out. I am going out to be among Jews who are still alive.

Commentary

No doubt this story gripped your heart as it did mine. While it is fiction, it is profoundly true, a slice of our history. As one who lived through the Nazi period, I know the grim way it was for so many Jews. All my relatives on my father's side were killed by the Nazis. If my father had not run away to America earlier, I might have faced a fate similar to that of the young man in the story.

Hitler shadowed and shaped my boyhood even within the safety of the United States. I remember telling myself at the age of fourteen that if people can be pushed around and killed merely for being Jews, we fortunate American Jews must devote our lives to making our people safe, secure, and free in a Jewish homeland or anywhere else we choose to live.

For me, this commitment to survival was easy to make; for the boy in our story, such a commitment to survival was virtually hopeless. What could keep alive his hope and faith? In fact, he was sustained by his religious convictions—but he acted upon his faith quite differently from his father.

Poppa, it seems, blamed the Jewish fighters more than he blamed the Nazis for his suffering. His religion turned him into a zombie, a man without will and without speech, relying only on God's will, rather than human action, for salvation. However, we should not judge Poppa too harshly; perhaps the story is unfair to him. After all, who kept the Jewish people and its faith alive through the centuries, those who tended the Torah and the religious spirit or those who, like Bar Kochba, chose war and rebellion?

But the boy in the story was inspired, like Bar Kochba, to fight back, and so he joined the Warsaw Ghetto freedom fighters. Certainly, in Jewish history, there have been few braver episodes than this—a poorly armed, tiny, untrained army hurling itself against a vast war machine and stopping it in its tracks for four weeks! But the uprising against the Nazis was doomed from the start; its end was certain suicide. Did it, therefore, make sense to fight?

For an answer to this question, we must consider the nature of the enemy. In a normal war, to fight and die against hopeless odds can be stupid. The Jewish commandment to "choose life" could well mean surrender; many wise military leaders have had to surrender at some point. But surrender by the Jews to the Nazis meant certain death, extermination in the camps. Perhaps it was better to die killing the killers themselves.

There is an even deeper question here. Where was God? How could a God of history have stood by in silence while the Jewish people were butchered? While Poppa believed that the Holocaust was God's way of punishing us for our sins, most readers would find such an idea repulsive. So perhaps our idea of God is wrong. Perhaps God does not shape human history. Perhaps God gave us free will so that we can determine the course of human events for good or for bad. If human beings were responsible for Nazism, then blaming God is a cop-out. It is easier to blame God than to judge how the entire world, the presidents, popes, the United States, the Soviet Union, England, France, Catholics, Protestants, Moslems—everybody including world Jewry—acted in the face of this monumental human catastrophe.

How to view God after Auschwitz—this question troubles our best thinkers. How to view the human conscience that is the core of our humanity—this looms as an ever larger and more painful question.

The story makes us wonder: Were the Nazis human beings, the creation of God? In Judaism, every human being is considered stamped in the image of God. No people is better than another in God's eyes. "Is your blood any redder than that of your enemies?" asks our tradition. "To Me, O Israelites, you are just like the Ethiopians." But if all human beings are the children of God, then what of the Nazis? Were they monsters? Freaks of history? How could God's children be so evil as to become the exterminators of whole groups of other human beings? The world still has no answers—only questions.

Yet we do know some things. We know that Nazi anti-Semitism built itself up one step at a time. Nazi Germany's Nuremberg Laws, adopted in 1935, denied Jews the right to do business, to go to school, to leave the country. If the German people had resisted these early anti-Jewish steps, the worldwide destruction that followed might have been averted. But most Germans were swept up by Hitler's racist rhetoric, and those who disagreed were afraid to speak up. Moreover, the rest of the world remained silent; virtually nobody assumed responsibility. Evil takes place when good people do nothing.

Pastor Martin Niemoller captured this idea in his famous statement: "In the thirties in Germany, when they came for the Communists, I didn't speak up because I wasn't a Communist. Then they came for the Jews, and I didn't speak up because I wasn't a Jew. Then they came for the trade unionists, and I didn't speak up because I wasn't a trade unionist. Then they came for the Catholics, and I didn't speak up because I wasn't a Catholic. Then they came for me, and by that time there was no one left to speak up."

Evil must be nipped in the bud. If the early American settlers had challenged the persecution of the Indians, the later massacres of Indians might have been averted. Even in our personal lives, the price of being human is to take responsibility.

How could an ordinary German became a Nazi? Hitler was a brilliant manipulator. He knew how to appeal to the fondest emotions of the German people. Nazism promised to restore German glory, taking revenge on the Allies who defeated Germany in World War I. A "racially pure" Germany, said the Nazis, would change human history, and the Nazi state would endure for a thousand years, built on the ashes of its enemies—Communists, Jews, Gypsies, gays. . . . With martial music stirring the blood, with mass rallies and hysterical speeches by Hitler, with violent suppression of all dissent, with visions of "the new order" dancing in their heads, most Germans were caught up in the excitement. It takes great courage to say no when everyone is saying yes. It took great courage to defend Jews when a whole nation was shouting, "Heil, Hitler!"

Even in America, I have seen the fever of public opinion rise like a tide, and I can testify from personal experience how hard it is to think for oneself. In World War II, I was a naval officer in the Pacific. My ship was smashed by a Japanese kamikaze pilot. I remember my fierce hatred of "the yellow Japs." I stood on that flaming ship, where some of my shipmates were killed, and I made a silent vow: "I will always hate the Japs." It was a foolish vow, one I have long since renounced. The Japanese, like the Germans, are now our allies and friends. I now drive a Subaru, watch television on my SONY, and eagerly look forward to visiting Japan some day.

But my hatred then was so strong that I actually welcomed the dropping of atomic bombs on the Japanese cities of Hiroshima and Nagasaki in 1945. Today, as an American, I have deep pangs of guilt about that horror, and I wonder over and over whether we had the right to do it. Beyond the question of the justice of our action, however, I have learned to judge people—Japanese, Germans, Arabs, Jews, Americans, whomever—as individuals and not as groups. How many evils could be avoided if we all stopped putting racial groups into categories and instead judged each person on individual merit!

Jews must always remember the Holocaust—but without laying guilt by association upon *all* Germans, including those born after the Holocaust itself. For people my age, whose lives were seared —and especially for the survivors themselves—this is painfully difficult. For young people, on the other hand, it may be too easy.

When President Ronald Reagan, in 1985 visited the Bitburg cemetery and honored the German war dead—including forty-seven members of the hated SS, special killers of Jews—old wounds were reopened, and we feared that the process of forgetting was underway. It is possible for a holocaust to be swept away as if it had never happened. Up to the beginning of World War I, the Armenians were the victims of a holocaust—massacres and slaughter—by the Turks. Yet the world has largely forgotten this crime. Is it possible that some day the Holocaust of the Jews similarly will be lost to memory? If so, what difference would that make? What exactly is the value of remembering? How should we Jews best memorialize the Holocaust to assure that such a catastrophe will never happen again?

Like author Lawrence Bush and me, you are among the lucky and the blessed. You live in a free and decent land. But even this free and decent America did not do much to rescue the Jews who stood on the lip of that Nazi volcano. If a holocaust erupted again, destroying some other group, would we Jews have the guts to join the resistance, to hide the hunted in our own homes, to brave the fury of bigots no matter how dangerous? Nobody knows until a moment of truth arrives. But we do know that to be Jewish means to be co-partners with God in saving people from suffering and death.

Rooftop Secrets

The USSR—Union of Soviet Socialist Republics—is often referred to as "the Soviet Union" or "Russia," just as the United States is nicknamed "America." Like America, the Soviet Union is a world superpower. In land area, it is the largest country in the world, and its population is over 275 million—a little more than the American population. Two million Soviet people are Jewish, comprising the third largest Jewish community in the world, after the U.S. and Israel.

Before 1917, Russia was a very poor, backward country, despite its great size. Its government was dictatorial, headed by a very powerful ruler called a czar. The Russian people in the great majority lived in poverty and misery, and the Jews of Russia were harshly persecuted. (See the introduction to "Blood Sisters.") Anti-Semitism and violence against Jews were very much a part of the fabric of Russian culture.

The Russian Revolution in 1917 overthrew the czar and, following a four-year civil war, established the first communist government in the world. This government promised many changes in the Russian way of life, including the abolition of anti-Semitism, which was to be accomplished by educating the peasants and making anti-Jewish activities illegal.

For a decade after the revolution, the promise was kept. Jewish culture, especially Yiddish culture, blossomed throughout the land. Judaism itself did not fare so well, for the new government was anti-religious in its general policy. But the anti-Semitic restrictions of the czarist era were abolished—for the time being.

In the 1930s, anti-Semitism reappeared with a vengeance in

98

Russia. Joseph Stalin, the dictator for over twenty-five years, trampled the flower of Soviet Yiddish culture, nearly destroying it. Stalin died in 1953, after killing many millions of his people. We shall see, however, that Soviet anti-Semitism did not die with him. That's why this story takes place neither under Stalin nor under a czar, but closer to the present. Anti-Semitism is still an uncured disease in Russia.

Jews in the Soviet Union are considered to be not simply a religious group but a "national minority," one of many minority groups recognized in the Soviet Union. According to the principles of the 1917 Revolution, these groups are to be treated with special care and respect. They are supposed to have their own languages, their own schools, their own books, their own culture, and some control over their own lives. In reality, the opposite is true. Minority groups in the Soviet Union are treated with suspicion by the government and their rights are often ignored. For the Soviet Jews, the situation is especially bad:

• Israel is looked upon by the Soviet government as an enemy country. Zionism is considered evil, and all Zionist organizations in the country are outlawed. Any Jew who cares about Israel—as most Jews naturally do—is treated with great suspicion.

• Soviet anti-Zionism also produces suspicion against anyone studying Hebrew. In fact, Soviet law makes it very difficult to study the language unless you are a scholar. Many teachers of Hebrew have been arrested.

• There are no Jewish history books published in Russia. It is extremely difficult for Jews to learn about the history and culture of their people.

• Almost no rabbis are being trained in the Soviet Union. The Jewish community is without leadership.

• Anti-Semitic writings are often published. Since *all* publishing in Russia is government-controlled, these writings must be government-approved.

As a result of these and other policies, Jews are cut off from their identities and forced to blend in, to assimilate with the general

Russian culture. Those who resist assimilation, displaying Jewish pride and seeking Jewish knowledge, face serious trouble.

In the early 1970s, a movement to leave the USSR developed among Soviet Jews. At that time, their cause became the cause of Jews all over the world. Our story occurs in a year when several thousand Jews were permitted to leave Russia, despite government policy that generally allows almost nobody to leave.

This Jewish emigration movement has brought thousands of Soviet Jews to Israel and America. However, for those Jews who stay behind, either by choice or because they can't get out, life has become harder. Many young Jews are no longer allowed to study science or mathematics in college because the government fears that these Jews will eventually leave the Soviet Union and bring their special skills to Israel or America. The heroine of our story is such a young Jew, Tanya Rubina, who hopes to become a cosmonaut (a Soviet astronaut). Her dream is threatened by anti-Semitism, and she begins to change from a star-gazing Russian to a soul-searching Jew.

Moscow, USSR: 1971

There are not many stars to be seen in the night sky over Moscow. As in most big cities, the lights from the streets and buildings are too bright to allow the stars' dim twinkling to shine through. But Tanya Rubina loved to go to the roof of her apartment building and watch the sky, anyway.

Usually, if her homework was done and the night air was not too cold, her parents allowed her to go up there. They knew that Tanya wanted with all her heart to be a cosmonaut. They had even bought her a telescope, though in Moscow it wasn't good for much more than gazing closeup at the moon or at other apartment windows. Tanya's parents also knew that, as a girl of fourteen, she sometimes needed to get out of the room that she shared with her grandmother, Bubbe Ruchel. The Rubina family, like most families in Moscow, lived in a small, crowded apart-

ment. In fact, Tanya's twelve-year-old brother, Yosef, had no room of his own but slept each night on the living room couch.

This evening, however, as on many Fridays, the Rubinas had dinner guests. Mrs. Haikin, who taught in the same high school as Tanya's mother, had come with her husband and their son, Gregor, who was Yosef's age. Tanya was not so sure that her parents were going to let her go to the roof tonight. Worse, she was afraid that Yosef and Gregor would be sent up there with her, which would spoil the feeling of being alone. But maybe if she asked permission at just the right moment . . .

She listened carefully to the grownups' conversation—mostly dull complaints about work, about empty shelves in department stores, about everyday annoyances. It was boring talk, boring enough to put Bubbe Ruchel to sleep in her chair and to make Yosef and Gregor fidget and kick each other under the table like little kids. Tanya, however, was a patient girl who liked nothing better than to play with her own imagination. She pretended that her parents and their guests were visitors from other planets, whose languages she was trying to understand. By doing this, Tanya managed to stay with the conversation—and meanwhile Mrs. Haikin grew a third eye in the middle of her forehead and Mr. Haikin's chin grew to a long point!

Then Tanya's father began to talk about the family's summer vacation plans. Tanya saw her chance to turn the conversation to her topic. "I'm going to the Young Pioneers camp for cosmonauts!" she announced proudly.

"You've *applied* to go," her father reminded her. "You haven't yet been accepted."

"Oh, but I will be," she said confidently. "I got the highest grades in my class in physics *and* chemistry!"

"You also have to remember," her mother said, "that the camp is not only for cosmonauts. There are many jobs in the Soviet space program besides just flying the ships."

"*Just* flying the ships!" Tanya repeated. "How can you say 'just'? What could be better than being a cosmonaut?"

"Oh, you might be an engineer, like your father," Mrs. Rubina said. "Or a computer scientist, or even the one who does the countdown. I don't know, darling. I just don't want you to feel disappointed because you've set your goals too high."

"Anyway," Yosef chimed in, "I never heard of a Jewish cosmonaut."

There was an awkward silence at the table. Tanya tried to think of something to say to her bratty brother—but then she heard her grandmother snoring softly, just as she snored in her bed in Tanya's room each night. It was a sound that made Tanya want to scream.

"Tanya," her mother said, "let's eat, all right? Enough with the . . ."

The girl stood, banging her chair. "Please excuse me," she said as politely as she could. Without waiting for permission, she walked to the door, declaring: "I'll be on the roof."

Mr. Rubina sighed as the door closed. "Our daughter," he explained to his guests, "has great dreams of outer space—while our son dreams only of living space, a room of his own. Eh, Yosef?"

Mr. Haikin replied in a low, sly voice: "We all have our dreams of more space . . . more freedom. . . ."

His wife patted his hand to hush him. "Perhaps," she suggested to Tanya's parents, "you shouldn't try to discourage her. If she is going to suffer discrimination because she's Jewish, there's nothing . . ."

"Oh, nonsense!" Mrs. Rubina interrupted. "It has nothing to do with nationality! It's just that many, many children apply to this camp."

"Many, many children apply," Mr. Haikin said gently, "and fewer and fewer Jewish children get in. We must face the facts. Our children are being excluded from certain professions, especially the sciences."

"But the Soviet constitution," Mrs. Rubina argued, "states that anti-Semitism is against the law!"

"And the Ten Commandments," her guest replied, "forbid us to worship idols—but even while Moses was on Mt. Sinai receiving the tablets, his people down below were worshiping a golden calf."

"Why are you telling us this religious foolishness?" she said.

"I'm afraid that it's no more a religion, and no more foolish, than is your faith in the Soviet constitution."

Suddenly Bubbe Ruchel interrupted, in a voice that gave no sign that she'd been napping. "If you children would stop arguing about what is happening and would *make* something happen . . ."

"What do you mean, Momma?" asked Tanya's father, relieved to have his wife's argument with Mr. Haikin interrupted.

The old woman leaned her elbows on the table. "When you were a boy," she said, "in the days of Stalin, and with the armies of Hitler ready to swallow Moscow—still, when Friday night came, we lit Sabbath candles. We didn't pretend, as you and your nice friends pretend, that Friday is simply the end of the week. Who knew when a week began or ended in the days of the war? But for us, Friday meant *Shabbos,* even if we had only potatoes to eat. You and your brothers were reminded every week that you were Jewish. But when I look at my granddaughter . . ." Bubbe Ruchel shook her head sadly. "Tanya has nothing to remind her of her heritage except an old Jewish *bubbe* who takes up too much room. But maybe, if you lit Sabbath candles, Tanya would not have to spend her nights looking for candles in the sky!"

Even as Bubbe Ruchel was saying this, Tanya was strolling across the roof of her building, admiring the apricot-colored sky. The days, she observed, were getting longer, and she knew why: because of the earth's tilt towards the sun, which brought more light and heat to the northern countries. In a month would be the solstice, June 22, the first day of summer and the longest day of the year. "I guess I'll hear about my application before then," Tanya thought. "But what am I going to do all summer if I'm not accepted?"

Tanya stretched her arms over her head and sighed. Oh, to fly away on the wings of night! To soar above the tallest buildings in Moscow, above the lights and noise and doubts and snores and bratty brothers! To see the earth from out there in the darkness, a bright, blue ball floating in the heavens. She would take great, weightless leaps across the surface of the moon. She would become heavier than an elephant on the giant planet Jupiter. She would skate along the rings of Saturn, catch a comet by its tail and ride it like a roller coaster! No, these thoughts were not all scientific, though Tanya did know all the facts there were to know about the planets and their moons, the sun and stars beyond. But her imagination went past facts—her imagination was the imagination of poetry:

> I want to fly above this earth,
> Above this separation,
> Into good or bad, happy or sad,
> Russian or Jew, country or nation.

In fact, Tanya *was* a poet, though nobody else knew it. She kept all her writing in one notebook, the same book in which she jotted down her observations of the sky each night. Usually there was little to say about the Moscow sky besides how the moon looked, and the notebook would have been mostly empty if not for Tanya's imagination, which always took her beyond what she could see with her eyes.

She kept the book hidden and dry near the chimney, inside an old milk crate. Now she went to get it, to write down the poem that was being born in her mind.

There was a boy sitting on her milk crate, reading a book of his own. "Oh," Tanya said, "hi," for she recognized him as a kid from school, although she had never learned his name.

Her voice startled him. He slammed shut his book and almost stood up, but controlled his fright at the last second and remained on the milk crate. "Hello," he said.

Tanya didn't really wish to be friendly, only to make sure that this boy didn't discover her secret hiding place and blab the news all over school. "I've got a telescope downstairs," she said. "You want me to get it? It makes the moon look as close as your nose and as big as your dinner plate!" Of course, she expected him to say yes, eagerly; while she had him staring through the telescope, she would sneak out her notebook behind his back.

But to Tanya's surprise, the boy's answer was a polite no.

"Oh, you're crazy," she teased. "Really, it's a great sight."

"I'm not so interested in the moon," he replied. "I'm more interested in other places."

"Oh? Like where? What are you reading, anyway?" She was close enough to see that he had a finger stuck inside his book, marking his place. So he was as anxious to get rid of her as she was to get rid of him!

"It's just a book," he said.

" 'Just a book,' " she mimicked him. "That's like saying that your girl friend is 'just a girl'."

"Look," he said, annoyed with her, "I'm trying to read. Okay?"

"Okay, okay!" Tanya clucked her tongue and gave up her plan. "But I'm trying to do something too, and it's underneath you. Do you mind standing up for a minute?"

He did as she asked and watched with surprise as she fetched her notebook. "I guess I can say goodbye to this as a hiding place," Tanya said sadly.

"What have you got there?"

"Oh, just a book." And now she was close enough to see *his* book. It was a worn, old volume with a title in Hebrew letters! She couldn't read them, but she recognized them as she would have recognized Chinese, Arabic, or English. "You read Hebrew?" she asked. "I never knew anyone who could."

He hushed her with a gesture, then looked around as if the neighboring buildings had ears or spies watching from every window. "Well," Tanya whispered, "it looks like we both have secrets."

"It's not a secret, really," the boy confessed. "Not any more. My family has applied to emigrate to Israel."

"Israel!" Tanya cried, then silenced herself with a hand over her mouth.

"Yes, Israel!" he said with fierce pride. "Why, do you believe all the lies they tell about Israel, as if it were the worst country in the world since Nazi Germany?"

"No, I . . . I don't know." She felt confused by his passion. "But don't you like it here?"

The boy looked at her closely. "It's more that 'here' doesn't like me," he said. "Tell me, are you Jewish?"

Tanya nodded. "But I'm not religious or anything," she said. "It's just my nationality. My grandmother sometimes forgets who she's talking to and tries to talk to me in Yiddish, but . . . Anyway, I've never had trouble for being Jewish."

"No," the boy said sadly, "you don't have trouble for being Jewish until you start to make something out of being Jewish. For me, that began two years ago when my family decided that I should become bar mitzvah. . . ."

"What's that?" Tanya asked.

He made a face that she didn't like at all, a look of surprise at her ignorance. "It's a special ceremony to show that a Jewish boy has come of age in the Jewish community."

"What about Jewish girls?" she said sharply.

He nodded. "Some Jews do it for girls, too. It happens when you're thirteen years old. You have to study Hebrew and learn to read from the Torah. . . ."

Tanya shrugged. "I don't know what that means either."

"Sure you do! The Torah? The Five Books of Moses?"

"You mean the Bible?"

"Yes. The Jews call the first five books of the Old Testament the 'Torah.' There," he said with a smile, "now you know a little Hebrew yourself."

"Very funny," Tanya said. "Now go on with your story." By now she was really interested. "Did you do that bar mitzvah thing?"

"Sure I did."

"So what kind of trouble did you have?"

"Simple," said the boy. "How do you think you find a Hebrew teacher in a country where there are no rabbis? People who teach

Hebrew are usually people who've been fired from better jobs because they applied to emigrate. And that means that they're teaching Hebrew illegally—without a license. So when you join a study group, and the police are watching your teacher, you end up being watched, too."

"And that's why you study up here?" Tanya said.

He nodded. "Hopefully your beloved moon up there is not a spy." He sighed and sat again on the milk crate. "My teacher was arrested just before my thirteenth birthday last year. All the kids who were studying Hebrew with him were kicked out of the Young Pioneers."

"You're kidding!" Tanya cried. "But the Young Pioneers are for everybody!"

"And how. You belong whether you want to or not. By the way," he added, "in Israel there are many different Jewish youth organizations—and you don't *have* to belong to any of them."

"So what?" Tanya argued. "There's no Soviet law that says you *have* to join the Pioneers. It's just . . ."

"Just a way to become a good Soviet citizen, huh?"

What a sarcastic kid! "No," Tanya said. "It's a way to have fun! Don't you like the Pioneers? I sure do. I've even applied to go to cosmonaut camp this summer."

He shook his head. "And what are you going to do all summer after you get rejected?"

"Thanks a lot!"

The boy shrugged. "Hey, don't blame me. If you want to make aliyah to the moon, that's your business. But you're going to have to build your own spaceship—unless your father's name is Boris Volynov."

"Who's he?"

"The first and only Jewish cosmonaut! And the last one, I bet."

"Oh, what do you know?" Tanya muttered. Then, after a pause, she said, "What's his name again?"

"Boris Volynov."

Just wait until she told Yosef!

"And what's your name?" the boy asked.

Tanya smiled and drew on the tar with her toe. "I haven't yet decided if I want to tell you."

He folded his arms. "Fine. But I'll make a deal with you, okay, Boris? If you get accepted to your camp before my family gets a visa to make aliyah . . ."

"What's that word?" Tanya asked. "More Hebrew?"

"Yeah. It means, like, to go up. People say it when they talk about going to Israel, as if Israel is a heavenly place, you know what I mean? So look," he continued, "if you get to your camp before I get to Israel, I'll buy you something—a radio! They send radio signals to other planets, right? So maybe you'll hear a broadcast from the Martians or something."

"Very funny."

"And if you win," he said, "you buy me . . . let's see . . . a yarmulke!"

"A what?"

"A yarmulke!" he repeated. "If you can't find one, you'll knit me one!"

"I don't even know what it is!" Tanya wailed.

"So ask your grandmother. Is it a deal?"

"Deal," she agreed. "Except that I don't know how to knit either."

"Well," he said, "ask your grandmother about that too." Then he stood and bowed. "Goodnight, Boris."

Tanya nodded gracefully. "Goodnight, Mr. Bar Mitzvah."

She sat on her milk crate, opened her notebook, and listened to his footsteps fading on the staircase to the apartments below. For an hour she sat there, quietly watching the night deepen, thinking about the boy's story, feeling his loneliness. How could he want to leave Mother Russia? It must have been a very deep hurt, deeper than dismissal from the Young Pioneers, that would cause his family to leave home. "And not only to leave home," she thought, "but to go to Israel—tiny, troubled Israel, where there are always wars!" Tanya had often heard, in school and on the street, the propaganda that Jews who wanted to emigrate from Russia were just money-grubbers, idiots who expected to get rich in the capitalist countries. "Well, maybe that's true of a few," Tanya now thought, "but to leave your homeland, your friends, your way of life, just to make money! I don't believe that most people would do that. *He* wouldn't, I bet," she thought, thinking again of the boy.

Tanya cupped her hands around her eyes to block out some of the light from the surrounding buildings. She could see a couple of stars twinkling out there, very faintly. She knew that there were millions, billions more of them, in the Milky Way and in other galaxies—and she wanted to see them, to be among them. "But is it really that I want to be out there," she wondered, "cramped inside a little space capsule? Or is it more that I want to be out of here, where I'm cramped by all the rules? It's funny how we're the biggest country in the world and yet it feels so cramped living here! Oh, but you better keep these thoughts to yourself, young lady, or you'll never get to cosmonaut camp!"

Tanya wondered if the boy, who had been reading his Hebrew book with the same eagerness with which she watched the stars, would ever see his goal fulfilled. Then she tried to put him out of her mind. He was, after all, going to be leaving. And it certainly wouldn't help her achieve *her* goal if she were known to be friends with someone who had been kicked out of the Young Pioneers. "The less I say about being Jewish," Tanya thought, "the better. He's just a Zionist anyway." She even tried to provoke herself into feeling angry at him. People like him were making things so difficult for people like her! But she could find no anger in her heart, only sadness at the memory of him slamming shut his precious book at the sound of her voice.

When she came downstairs again, Tanya found her grandmother lying in bed. On a table next to her bed, two white candles were burning. "What's with the candles?" Tanya asked. "You want some light, Bubbe?"

Tanya could hear a smile in her voice: "They give me all the light I need, thank you, darling."

"Okay. But make sure you don't burn the house down. Okay?"

"I've got plenty of experience with candles," Bubbe Ruchel assured her.

"Goodnight, then." But suddenly Tanya turned around and sat on the edge of her own bed. "Bubbe?" she said. "What's a yarmulke?"

Tanya did not see the boy again until the following Monday, when he got on her school bus. He had to stand as there were no seats left, and Tanya was stuck next to a window and could only wave. She did this, but only once, then reminded herself: Nobody else needed to know that they were friends. . . .

The boy waited for her as the bus unloaded in front of the school. "I think you're going to win our bet," he said after nodding hello. "My father was fired from his job on Saturday. They say that's a bad sign—our visa will probably be delayed or even denied."

"Oh, dear," Tanya said, glancing around to see who else was listening. She wanted to keep up with the other kids, not to be seen standing here with him.

"I think you could fly to the moon and back ten times in the time it'll take me to get to Israel," he said miserably.

That word, "Israel," threw Tanya into a panic. "Listen, I'm late."

"For what? Classes haven't even started."

"I've got to go!" she blurted, and quickly walked away without looking back. Her ears were ringing, and she couldn't tell if that was because he had said "Israel" in a loud voice or because she had been caught in her lie.

All day long she worried about meeting him in the halls between classes. Her fear came true as she was entering geography class. She saw him as he lifted his face from a water fountain in the hallway. He saw her, too—but he seemed to look right through her. Tanya turned and stumbled into the classroom.

"Don't hurt yourself," said her teacher, Mrs. Stanislava. "It won't improve your grade."

"Sorry," Tanya mumbled, rushing to her seat.

"Now, class, come to attention." Mrs. Stanislava tapped a pencil on her desk. The class became quiet immediately. "Today we're going to learn a lesson in internationalism by writing letters —messages of peace—to the heads of government of any country in the world. This will be our message." She turned and wrote in Russian on the blackboard:

We, the children of the Soviet Union, extend our hands in peace and friendship to the children of _____.

"You will fill in the blank with the name of the country you choose," Mrs. Stanislava explained. "Now, who can write this message on the board in English?"

Tanya tried to focus, to translate the message in her head. Instead, she was thinking about the old Hebrew book with its weird, handsome letters. The girl sitting next to her volunteered and managed to do the English with only a little bit of help from the teacher.

"Very good," Mrs. Stanislava said. Next she drew down the map of the world so that it covered the blackboard. "Now, one by one, I want you to stand, announce the country to which you're going to write, and then come up to the map and point to it. All right? We'll start with the first row of seats."

"Czechoslovakia," announced the first boy.

"Very good. And who is the head of government in Czechoslovakia?"

"President Ludvik Svoboda," the boy shouted back, "and the prime minister is Lubomir Strougal."

"Excellent. And now—the map."

The boy ran to the blackboard and poked his finger at the map.

"Cuba," said the next student.

"And the head of state?"

"Fidel Castro."

"Very good. Now the map."

Yugoslavia, Poland, Mozambique, Vietnam. . . . All of the children were naming countries that were allies of the Soviet Union. "What about the United States?" Leah thought. "What about Mexico? France? England? Brazil? Zimbabwe? China? Egypt? And Israel—what about Israel?"

"Afghanistan," said another pupil. "Hungary," said the next. "Rumania." "Angola."

What about Israel?

Tanya squeezed her lips shut. "Don't say it, dummy!" she pleaded with herself. "Just bite your tongue, and someday you'll get to see the whole earth from outer space, all the countries blended into one beautiful planet. . . ." And she imagined herself, back from a space voyage, riding in a parade as thousands of people tried to get a look at her. . . .

But that boy from the roof, that boy in the hall—he would look right through her. He would look as if she weren't even there.

"Syria," said the boy in the seat ahead of Tanya.

And now it was her turn. Everyone was looking at her as she stood. Tanya wished her desk were a rocketship so she could blast off and fly right through the ceiling. "All aboard!" she would shout to that boy on the roof, that boy in the hall, that boy in her head. "All aboard, Mr. Bar Mitzvah!"

"Israel," she heard herself say out loud, though she knew it was crazy as she saw the eyes of her classmates popping like flashcubes in a camera. Their faces all turned to Mrs. Stanislava. Tanya walked quickly to the map. Israel, one of the smallest countries in the world, would take a long time to find.

Commentary

In our story of Jewish life in the USSR, Tanya's naming of Israel in the classroom could be very costly.

It might very well shatter her hope of being accepted to the summer camp of her choice. Almost certainly, her action doomed her dream of becoming a cosmonaut. In Soviet propaganda, Israel is portrayed as a warlike, imperialistic state whose land was stolen from its rightful owners, the Arabs. In fact, the Soviets often describe Israel as a "Hitlerite, Nazi state"—the ugliest and most insulting description possible. Tanya's teacher would be expected to report to the authorities Tanya's pro-Israel sentiment. That information on Tanya's record would certainly prevent her from fulfilling her hopes.

Why did Tanya do it? What impulse motivated her to pick Israel? Obviously, she was affected by "Mr. Bar Mitzvah," the boy she met on the roof. He was dedicated to learning Hebrew, practicing Judaism, and trying to make aliyah at great personal sacrifice. What miracle inspired such Jewish dreams in his heart, considering that he grew up in a country where there are no rabbis, no seminaries, no Jewish schools, where religion is despised, and where Judaism and Zionism are treated by the Communist authorities with contempt and persecution?

The reappearance in 1948 of a Jewish state touched a sensitive nerve among Soviet Jews. When Golda Meir came to Moscow as Israel's first ambassador, thousands of Jews flooded the streets to sing and dance and touch this representative of a living Jewish people. In 1967 when Israel was invaded by Arab armies, threatening another holocaust, Jews in the USSR hung on every word they could hear from their radios or from the whispered news from friends. To them, it was *their* people who stood in jeopardy; *their* brothers and sisters who fought back with such courage and dignity; *their* destiny that was being shaped on the battlefield and in the growth of a proud Jewish state. Thus, a fierce yearning for Jewish expression and a fervent Zionism swept through segments of Soviet Jewry, touching off a Jewish movement which caught the whole world by surprise.

That movement immediately faced official anti-Semitism—arrests, persecution, school quotas, loss of jobs, and bans on the teaching of Hebrew and Zionism. Yet none of this has been able to break the back of the Jewish resistance movement in the Soviet Union. Hundreds of thousands of Soviet Jews have made their way to Israel or the United States, and even more struggle against odds to sustain their Jewish identities in Russia while waiting for the iron gates to open and let them out.

The vision of Israel kindled the Jewish flame in the silent tomb of the USSR. Perhaps that vision will transform the life and dreams of our Tanya, who might, one day, fulfill her aspirations to be a space pioneer—but in Israel.

In America, we have the freedom to be what we want to be. Our religion is our own business. We can belong to a temple, attend a Jewish school, work with our rabbi (even plan to become one), learn Hebrew, visit Israel (or make aliyah if we choose), become a bar or bat mitzvah, read any book (or write one), and freely pursue our goals for the future. That's what freedom is all about. But when it is so easy to choose, many people choose nothing! Almost half the Jews in America belong to no synagogue and affiliate with no Jewish institution. Think about it! While we are free to choose, most Jews choose to do nothing to keep Jewish life alive. That is their right, of course—but does it mean that Jews have to suffer like Tanya or her friend to appreciate what our ancestors gave their lives to maintain? Is it human nature not to value something that, like freedom itself, we simply take for granted?

Imagine the unthinkable: our government closing down every synagogue and proclaiming Judaism and Zionism un-American. Would Jews simply go along, or would we fight back with all our strength? Would we shrug in resignation or embrace our Jewish lives with stubborn faith and renewed courage? Would we defy such persecution and take our schools underground? It is a sad commentary that people tend to take for granted the most important qualities of life—health, freedom, identity, and religious faith —until they are taken away or placed at risk.

What can we do to help Soviet Jews? Certainly we can pressure our president and Congress to raise the issue of Soviet anti-Semitism in any and all talks with the Soviet leadership. We can educate the public by joining in demonstrations, marches, vigils, sit-ins, walkathons, petition campaigns, and the variety of public events available to us. We can write to young Soviet Jews like Tanya and her friend and "twin" bar and bat mitzvahs with them. (Twinning is a system by which a bar or bat mitzvah in the U.S. shares his or her ceremony on behalf of a Soviet bar or bat mitzvah.) We can also reach out to Soviet Jews who now live in our communities and go to our temples and schools. If we are one Jewish people, we must never forget those who cannot speak for themselves. We must be their voice and their champion.

My wife and I had the privilege of visiting with Jews in Moscow and Leningrad. We met with young refuseniks (those who apply for visas to leave Russia but have been refused by the authorities) in their apartments. Most of them had been dismissed from their jobs. Some brilliant scientists and professionals had to work as janitors and streetsweepers. Many were harassed by the secret police and by neighbors. But all were determined to learn Hebrew, to study Judaism, and to wait until the political winds change and the gates are opened for them. Some have been waiting for years. Even when the authorities subject them to phony trials and send them to prison camps, they refuse to abandon their dreams. They are among the most heroic people I have met. They reminded me of the blacks with whom I worked in the Deep South of the United States during the civil rights era in the 1960s. Their quiet dignity and enduring faith are inspiring.

In my opinion, any real hope that Soviet Jewish dreams will be realized lies in an improvement in the tense relations between the United States and the Soviet Union. If the two superpowers can learn to live together despite their great differences, there is hope that the Soviets will ease their restrictions on Jewish emigration. An arms accord might warm up the climate and induce the Soviets to permit the exodus of those Jews who want to leave.

Obviously, many Jews would still choose to stay in Russia. After all, Jews have lived there for centuries—under the czars, under Stalin, and with all the anti-Semitism which darkened Jewish lives through the generations. Emigration is, therefore, not the only issue. An end to Soviet anti-Semitism would allow Jews who re-main in the USSR to practice their Judaism, train rabbis, educate their children, open synagogues, study Hebrew, and develop national organizations and institutions.

Perhaps it is too much to expect the Russians to practice American-style religious liberty. It is not too much, however, to insist that Jews be entitled at least to the same national and religious rights that other ethnic groups enjoy under the Soviet constitution.

The Visitor

World peace and progress through cooperation: these were the hopes of humanity when the United Nations was established as an international peace organization in 1945.

World War II, which had taken the lives of so many millions of people, including six million Jews, was over. The Nazi ambition to conquer the world had been smashed. It was hoped that the United Nations would prevent such a war from occurring ever again.

The underdeveloped countries of Asia and Africa that were dominated as colonies by England, France, and other European countries were demanding and gaining independence. It was hoped that the United Nations could help these new countries to prosper.

The massively destructive nuclear bomb, invented by the U.S. and dropped twice on Japan to end World War II, now threatened all life on earth. It was hoped that the United Nations would stop the spread of such weapons.

The United States and the Soviet Union, the two most powerful countries on earth, had fought together against the Nazis in the war. It was hoped that the United Nations could help these superpowers find a way to cooperate and settle their own differences peacefully.

Hunger, disease, and ignorance still plagued much of the world. It was hoped that the United Nations could help overcome these problems.

Unfortunately, despite the existence of the United Nations for over forty years, few of these hopes have come true. Wars continue to be fought all over the world. Newly independent countries struggle with poverty and dictatorship. Nuclear weapons have spread to other countries. The U.S. and the USSR have become deadly enemies who don't dare go to war with each other but haven't dared to make peace. And hunger, disease, and ignorance continue to ruin lives all over our planet.

Nonetheless, the United Nations has, at times, been successful as a kind of world government. One such success came in 1947, when the U.N. decided to divide the land of Palestine into two new nations: a Jewish state and an Arab state.

Why two states? The Arabs and Jews living in Palestine did not get along well enough to share the land peacefully. Why a Jewish state? The Holocaust had left the Jewish people desperately in need of a homeland, a place where they could live in safety and rebuild Jewish life from the ashes. Since the Zionist movement had already brought many Jews to Palestine, the holy land of Judaism, many Holocaust survivors wanted to go there. Why an Arab state? The Arabs living in Palestine were entitled to independence and control over their lives and their land. It was time for the people of Palestine to run their own lives.

In 1947, the plan to partition Palestine was adopted by the General Assembly of the United Nations with support from the world's most powerful countries. But the Arab countries surrounding Palestine, including Egypt, Syria, Iraq, and Jordan, immediately invaded the new Jewish state and tried to destroy it.

With great heroism and much sacrifice, the small Jewish state won the war and, in 1948, the State of Israel *was* established as the U.N. had ordered. But the Arab state never became a reality, and the Palestinian Arabs became refugees, people without a homeland, as a result of the war between Israel and its Arab invaders.

The Arab nations have never accepted Israel's right to exist in the Middle East; thus, in 1956, 1967, and 1973, Israel has had to fight wars with those nations. The Palestinians, too, have made war against Israel, using terrorism as their chief weapon. The Israelis, in turn, have refused to negotiate to create an independent Palestinian homeland. Years of war and hatred have resulted in one of the most complicated situations in the world:

• The Arab countries continue to threaten Israel. Only Egypt, in 1979, under President Anwar Sadat, has made peace with Israel. The other Arab nations use Israel as a scapegoat for their problems.

• The Palestinians are torn between those who want to negotiate with Israel in order to regain part of Palestine as a homeland and those who want to destroy Israel and take back *all* of Palestine.

• The Israelis are divided between those who want to seek peace with the Palestinians and those who want to defeat them with such military actions as the 1982 Israeli invasion of Lebanon.

• The rivalry between the U.S. and the USSR has become a part of the problem because the Soviet Union backs the Arabs and America backs the Israelis.

Perhaps the only successful solution to this complex problem can come from the United Nations—if the U.N. can bring together Israel, the Palestinians, the Arab countries, the U.S., and the USSR for peace talks. However, part of the Arab war against Israel has been a "propaganda" war, a war of words meant to isolate Israel from the friendship of other countries. Much of this propaganda war has been fought at the United Nations itself. In fact, the Arab members of the U.N. have tried more than once to get Israel expelled from the U.N.

On November 10, 1975, the war of words reached its worst stage when the General Assembly passed a "resolution," a statement of opinion, describing Zionism as "a form of racism." Instead of returning to the 1947 principle that both Jews and Palestinian Arabs deserve states of their own in the Middle East, the resolution was stating that Zionism itself, the very idea of a Jewish state, is evil.

Seventy-two countries voted for this resolution—just enough to make a majority. Why did so many vote unfairly against Israel? First, many countries, especially the underdeveloped Asian and African countries, needed Arab oil and would have voted for almost anything that the Arab nations wanted. Second, many countries were anti-American, mainly because of the unpopular U.S. war in Vietnam, and voted against Israel because Israel was America's ally. Third, there was enough anti-Semitic feeling in the world to fuel anti-Israel actions.

The "Zionism is racism" resolution made Jews all over the world feel isolated. They feared that anti-Semitism would spread again. It seemed that the world was turning against Israel and the Jewish people. Many Jews, including American Jews, contemplated aliyah to Israel to link their lives more closely to the Jewish state.

This story tells about a New York Jewish family, a divorced woman and her eleven-year-old son, that is forced to ponder this question in a very personal way.

New York City: 1975

"Leave me alone now, honey, I have to get ready." Diana blew a kiss to Eli and closed her bedroom door.

How often he had heard her say that! As his mother prepared to go to antiwar meetings, to civil rights marches, to meetings of her women's groups, there would come a point at which she said to Eli: "Leave me alone now, I have to get ready." Hearing those words and seeing her bedroom door closing always made Eli uneasy. It reminded him of those strange two months, many years ago, when Diana had left him with his father, Allen, and had gone off—disappeared, really—to Israel.

Eli had been only four years old at the time. His father had spent those two months in an angry mood, which only added to Eli's misery at "losing" his mother. Now, after years of talking with both his parents, and after a year of seeing Dr. Eisenoff, Eli had gotten used to having divorced parents. He knew that he was not the only kid at P.S. 58 who lived that way. He understood that his parents' split-up had not been his fault. He understood that he could still love them both without betraying either. Yet always, as Diana "got ready" for something, Eli would get that same old feeling in his stomach—a feeling that made him want to hug his belly or go to the bathroom.

"Our bodies develop habits," Dr. Eisenoff had told him, "that are much slower to change than our ideas. Think about how long it took you to stop biting your nails, even after you yourself thought it was a pretty ugly habit." "He's right," thought Eli, standing near his mother's door, "only this time my feeling's *not* just a habit." Diana, in fact, wasn't going out but was getting ready for a guest—a man named Avram, from Israel. He was coming for dinner, straight from the airport, and Diana was *very* nervous about it. All Eli knew was that she had met the guy on that trip to Israel, seven years ago.

"Ma!" Eli called at her door. "How come I feel like you're going someplace when you're not?"

Diana opened her door. She had finished dressing from the waist up but hadn't yet wrapped around her skirt. She looked like a dancer in black tights. Her bead earrings hung nearly to her shoulders. "Eli," she said, "how about starting to set the table for us?"

"You're changing the subject," he said, straying into her room. "Dr. Eisenoff says I shouldn't let you get away with that."

"Oh, yeah?" She began to brush her black, bushy hair. "Maybe Dr. Eisenoff would like to adopt you. He seems to say everything you want him to say. 'Dr. Eisenoff thinks I should have a bigger allowance. Dr. Eisenoff says . . .' "

"Cut it out!" Eli cried, hurt by his mother's sarcasm. "I don't do that! I never say things that he didn't say."

"Of course you don't, honey." Diana sat on the edge of her bed. "I'm sorry. I was just kidding."

"And you're still trying to change the subject," he said.

Diana folded her hands in her lap. "And what subject is that?"

Eli rubbed his belly. "I feel sick. I feel nervous. Who is this guy, anyway?"

His mother lost her smile and turned back to her mirror. "I want you to meet him without knowing everything about him, Eli."

"Why?"

"Because that's what *I'm* trying to do. I haven't seen Avram in years, and I want to get a new first impression of him, if that's at all possible." She caught Eli's eye in the mirror. "You know what I mean?"

He nodded, though he could tell from how beautiful Diana looked that this dinner meant more than a "first impression." Eli even began to feel a bit jealous, thinking, "If she can get a new impression of this guy, why not of Dad?" Then he remembered Dr. Eisenoff's advice: "It's fine for you to wish that your parents were still together, Eli. But don't expect your wishes to bring them together. Each of you has to feel what you're feeling and do what you need to do with your life."

The flutter in his stomach kicked up again. He almost asked his mother, "How come I'm not staying in Brooklyn tonight?" Often he went to his father's apartment when his mother had a date. But obviously this guy Avram was more than a date. "Just wait and see," Eli told himself.

"Okay, see you later," he said to Diana and went to set the table, making enough noise to let her know it was being done.

Avram was thirty-eight years old, chunky, and curly-headed. He was a reporter for the *Jerusalem Post* and would be spending the next few days at the United Nations. He had a suitcase and a portable typewriter with him. Eli realized that Avram was planning to spend the next few nights with him and his mother there on the Upper West Side of Manhattan.

They had not been together for seven years, yet Diana and Avram were quiet during dinner. Unlike most of Diana's boyfriends whom Eli had met, this one didn't seem to need to talk about himself, his work, his accomplishments. Diana seemed different at the table, too. Usually by now she would have said much more about her writing and her political beliefs and probably would have been involved in an argument. Instead it was Eli who did most of the talking.

By the end of the meal, Eli was asking questions about Israel and its wars with the Arabs. Avram, it turned out, had been a pilot in the Israel Defense Forces and had fought in the Six Day War and the Yom Kippur War without getting wounded. "But I *have* been wounded, you see," he told Eli while Diana served dessert. "In my heart I've been wounded—I've lost many friends to those wars. Every Jew in Israel, from the baby to the oldest, is a soldier, because for us every war is a matter of survival. Of course, for you," he added with a shrug, taking a cup of steaming coffee from Diana's hand, "my stories are very exciting, like *Star Wars* or something. But life in Israel is not a movie!"

"Eli's not a big fan of war movies," Diana said. "In fact, I bet you've been to more antiwar demonstrations than war movies, haven't you, honey?"

"Probably."

"But America itself is one big movie!" Avram insisted. "And for American Jews, being Jewish is like buying candy at the counter. That's all it means, and that's all the time it takes. Even his name . . ." Avram pointed to Eli. "The name of a great Hebrew prophet. Elijah! But the holiness is removed in America, and Elijah becomes Eli. Being a Jew here is like eating fast food all the time."

Diana leaned forward and sipped her coffee. She was holding back her anger, Eli could tell. Avram, too, buried his nose in his cup. To Eli they looked like a couple in the middle of a long, never-ending argument. He tried to think of something to say that would make them relax, but first Diana spoke up: "We should have saved this conversation for at least one day, Avram. After seven years apart, we should have allowed ourselves to have some fun first."

"I know," he said quietly.

"No, you don't," Diana replied. "Not really. You don't realize how insulting you are! Here I serve you a delicious dinner, and you tell me that my life as a Jew is a fast-food restaurant. Then I introduce you to my son, and you act as if I don't understand the name I gave him. So? Shall I insult you back? Shall I say that all Israeli men are conceited? Shall I tell you that Israeli Jews have no understanding of the *real* meaning of Judaism, the real feeling for social justice?"

Avram sat stiffly, like a soldier at attention. Diana hushed herself by biting her finger. Avram stood up. "I should leave," he said. "We can try again in a day or two. . . ."

Diana slapped the table, making the dishes rattle. "Don't you dare go anywhere!" she shouted. "Let's fight this out! We've spent seven years avoiding it. Besides," she added in a lower voice, suddenly smiling, "if you can't face *my* insults, how are you going to face the Arabs at the United Nations?"

Avram sighed and sat back down.

They had agreed to argue, yet they spent the rest of the evening as they had spent most of dinner, being quiet with each other and paying a lot of attention to Eli. Avram taught him how to play a Lebanese card game; Diana gave him seconds of dessert and allowed him to listen to a really obnoxious radio station on the stereo. Eli went to bed at 10 o'clock feeling as if he'd been at a birthday party. But as he lay in the dark, listening for sounds outside his door, he tried to figure out what Avram and Diana had been arguing about.

Jewishness: Diana never said much about it except when she was talking about political things. Neither she nor Allen were religious or active in Jewish organizations; they weren't giving Eli a Jewish education or planning for him to be bar mitzvah. Still, all the causes that Diana cared about and wrote about for magazines—the war in Vietnam, equality for women and minority groups, opposition to nuclear weapons, criticism of the government—these were connected, she often said, to the Jewish part of her. Eli remembered, for instance, the time he'd seen his mother crying over the *New York Times.* The newspaper had some horrible photographs of Vietnamese kids who'd been burned by napalm, a kind of firebomb dropped by American airplanes. "These pictures are like the Holocaust!" Diana had cried out loud. "It's like Auschwitz all over again! We've got to stop this war! These pictures are pictures of Jews!"

"Social justice," "the prophetic tradition," "freedom from slavery," "fear of anti-Semitism," "caring about your neighbors" —these were the words she used when the subject of being Jewish came up. Jewishness, for her, was a sort of feeling about the world, a caring feeling. But, for Eli, that didn't mean a whole lot. In fact, all of Diana's ideas—except, maybe, "fear of anti-Semitism"—weren't they simply what being *American* was supposed to be all about?

Eli thought and wondered and wondered and thought until his thoughts became dreams and he was fast asleep.

When he awoke, it wasn't yet morning. He heard his mother's and Avram's voices, and he figured out that they were in the living room. "Well," Eli thought, "I have to pee." Quietly he opened his door.

Passing through the hall to the bathroom, he caught a glimpse of his mother on the couch next to Avram. The living room lamplight made Eli squint. He peed in the dark in the bathroom. Obviously neither of the grownups had seen him, for they continued their discussion without lowering their voices. Eli didn't flush. He brought down the toilet seat and sat on it.

"How can it be that politics comes between us this way?" Avram was saying. "I cannot believe how we feel so close, and then end up in a political debate!"

Eli had to strain to hear his mother's reply: "Politics means more than the way you vote, Avram. Politics means who you are, how you live your life."

"But I love who you are, Diana. I just want you to live your life where you belong—you and Elijah—in Israel. In America, you'll always be just a visitor!"

Eli stiffened. "Israel?" he thought. "Is he crazy? What about my dad? What about my friends? Who wants to go to a foreign country. And my name is *Eli!*"

"We need women like you," Avram went on, "intelligent, passionate, caring. . . ."

"To say that you want me in Israel," said Diana, "is different from saying that my life in America is no good."

"I've already apologized for that," Avram said. "But I know that you will *not* come to Israel until you are made to see what's wrong with your precious America, why it cannot be your home."

"I know what's wrong with America!" Diana replied, interrupting. "I've put half of my life and *all* of my writing career into dealing with that very subject. There's racism in America. There's poverty. There's mistreatment of people."

"The same in Israel!" Avram said. "The same problems to solve—only there you are solving them on behalf of your *own* people."

Eli, now standing in the darkness by the bathroom door, listened for his mother's answer. He thought: "Mom better just tell him to forget it. I'd never go to Israel. Who wants to? God, is she, like, in *love* with this guy?"

"Avram," Diana said, "I'm an American. I'm not an Israeli. I don't speak Hebrew. I've only been there the time I met you."

"No excuse," Avram said. "Your grandmother never set foot in America until she ran away from the czar in Russia and came here. She learned a new language, too. So now it's your turn. Let your son grow up as a real Jew, not as a phony American!"

"Stop that!" Diana argued. "Who are you to say what a real Jew is? Or a real American? I mean, if there's any justice in this world, Avram, we *must* stay here. It's *my* tax dollars that have paid to bomb the Vietnamese all these years. I've got to make up for that. To me, *that's* what being Jewish is about—responsibility. It's my responsibility—and my son's—to heal America and make it a better place, a better home for Jews and for everybody!"

Avram said something in a low voice. Eli was relieved when Diana asked him to repeat it.

"*Tikun olam,* I said. It means the healing of the world." He sighed so loud that Eli could hear his breath. "All through history, my sweet Diana, Jews like you have been trying to heal the world, yes? Only to find out that the world doesn't want to be healed—and hates the Jews for trying!"

"Look, Avram," Diana said, "there's always someone who throws rocks at the prophets. Still, the prophets are the ones we care about and remember."

"Oh, sure," he said sarcastically. "We remember the prophets. We remember them because they're dead! And they're dead because they were too busy trying to save the world instead of saving themselves and their people. What about all those Jews in Europe before the Holocaust, Diana? Do you think they were so different from you? They laughed at the Zionists just the way you laugh at me."

"I'm not laughing at you, Avram!"

"They said, 'No, no, we mustn't go to Palestine. We are an international people. We have many different homelands; we are Germans, Poles, French . . . and in each country we will perform the work of *tikun olam.*' Beautiful!" Avram clapped his hands. "A beautiful idea! Only the Zionists were right, don't you see? My grandfather and his friends who went to Palestine in the 1920s —they were right. Because they understood that, if *they* didn't unite the Jews in one land, someone like Adolf Hitler would—in the land of Auschwitz! Hitler would come along and take all the good Jews and the bad Jews and the Jews who wanted to heal the world and the Jews who didn't give a damn and the Jews who had beautiful Jewish names and the Jews who shortened their names to Eli! He'd take them all and ship them to the gas chambers! There's the end result of your *tikun olam!* It'll be the same in America! You think you're safe because you're in New York, where there are so many Jews. But watch tomorrow night—watch the news on your television—watch what happens at the United Nations, that body of world peace, right here in New York. See how safe you feel once the Arabs start to vote!"

It took a long while for Diana to speak. Eli felt his whole body waiting for his mother to say something that would prove that Avram was wrong. He seemed to know so much about history and real life; he was a reporter and he had fought in two wars; he was a man and had a lot of experience. Could he be right about Jews not being safe?

But Diana knew how to argue really well. Diana would set it straight. . . .

"Calm down," she said at last. "I'm not attacking Israel, Avram. I'm glad to have Israel in this world, just as I'm glad, more than glad, to have *you* in this world. But *this* is my home. *This* is my safety. Israel is no protection against anti-Semitism, you know that. One little country can't do it all by itself. Israel just gives the anti-Semites a clearer target to shoot at! And the only way we're going to stop anti-Semitism is the same way we stopped Hitler in the end—by an international effort. We've got to get rid of all prejudice. We've *got* to heal the world!"

"You sound ridiculous," Avram grumbled, "like a starry-eyed teenager."

"Why?" she cried. "Because I say that we can't go running to Israel when there's work to be done right here? Who was he, that famous rabbi who said something about not just being for himself?"

" 'If I am only for myself, what am I?' " Avram recited. "Rabbi Hillel. But *first* he asked, 'If I am not for myself, who will be for me?' And *you*, Diana, are not for yourself. You think you're going to save the world, but you're not even ready to save yourself."

"I don't have to save myself!" Diana argued. "I'm not in danger! I'm an American! You *are* in danger, however, because you live in Israel! And *that's* why you think the way you do!"

"You're *not* an American!" Avram hollered. "You're a Jew! That's how the whole world thinks of you, including your fellow Americans! And you—you don't even know the name of Hillel!"

Now Eli wanted the argument to end. Let it be over! His mother sounded weak and afraid, angry without being right. Let it be over! Then Avram would be gone in the morning, and Eli would go to school, and Diana would go back to her work on the typewriter, and they could forget about this Jewish stuff. . . .

"Tomorrow," Avram said, as if he had heard Eli's thoughts, "is November 10th. In Germany, in 1938—the year before I was born—November 10th was the *Kristallnacht,* the night of broken glass. The Nazis went on a wild pogrom, burning synagogues, smashing Jewish stores and houses, beating and murdering Jews all over Germany. It was a rehearsal—a rehearsal for the Holocaust."

There was a silent pause. Eli wondered if Avram was crying. "Hitler wanted to see what the world would do for the Jews." No, his voice was clear—and coming closer to the bathroom! "The world did nothing. Well, tomorrow is November 10th, and the Arabs at the United Nations will make a pogrom with words. They want to see what the world will do for the Jews. . . ."

Eli froze. Avram was standing right outside the bathroom, groping for the light switch on the wall.

"And the world," he murmured, "will do nothing, my love."

The bathroom light blazed on. Eli stood, blinking and shame-faced, in front of the sink. He expected Avram to shout in surprise, to jump, or even hit him out of reflex like a nervous soldier frightened by a sound.

Avram's eyes were blue pools of tears. He stepped over to the medicine cabinet mirror and touseled Eli's hair. "I love your mother, you know that?"

Eli wordlessly slipped out the door.

All the next day he felt strange at school—strange because it was a normal, usual day. Nobody talked about that night in Germany in 1938; nobody talked about the United Nations and what was going on there. Even during social studies, when they discussed current events, all the talk was about President Nixon and the Watergate scandal and other news.

Yet so many kids in Eli's sixth-grade class were Jewish! So was Mrs. Bergman, his teacher! Some of the kids went every day to

Hebrew school. "They're even more Jewish than me," Eli thought. "So why isn't anyone saying anything or even thinking anything? Don't they know what's going on? Aren't they scared?"

Well, Eli asked himself, why was *he* not saying anything either? Why not raise his hand and say, "Mrs. Bergman, there's something very important about this day, and we should be talking about it . . ."?

Yeah, but what if she said, "Tell the class, Eli."

He would say: "Well, uh, this Israeli guy . . . uh . . ."

"I just don't know enough!" Eli said to himself, slumping in his chair. "I don't know *anything* about being Jewish—not really!"

He thought about what Avram had said about danger, about not being American, about the Holocaust, about loving Diana, things that had caused this man, this soldier, to cry. Eli thought: "Maybe I don't *want* to know about those things. Maybe in America we *can* forget about it." But he knew that he was lying to himself to feel better. He kept on thinking about Avram's blue, teary eyes.

Suddenly he wished his mother would come to get him out of school. It was his oldest school feeling—as if he were back in kindergarten—the feeling that he didn't want to learn, to grow up, to think. He wanted Diana. He wanted her to leave her work aside and come for him. He wanted to be home, the only safe place in the world. . . .

She wasn't there when he got home. He found a note telling him that supper was in the refrigerator and she'd be home at seven. Eli had a nervous stomach; he didn't feel like eating. He spent a long time looking out the window, watching the sky get dark, watching the city lights come up. Was he nervous just because his mother was out—out, probably, with Avram, and talking about going to Israel? No, there was more to it. There was the date itself: November 10th. Avram had called it the night of broken glass. Eli could imagine bombs falling on New York, knocking over buildings, shattering windows—bombs not just for Jews, but for everyone. Nuclear bombs. Maybe Nixon would go crazy because of Watergate and push the button.

He turned on the television for company. He watched the news from six to seven, switching among the main channels. There was nothing about the United Nations. There was nothing, really, but commercials. Eli felt as if someone were teasing him.

Diana called at seven. "Honey," she said, "I'm going to be late. I'm sorry. I'm at the Isaiah Wall, waiting for Avram."

"What's the Isaiah Wall?" asked Eli.

"Oh! I'll have to bring you here sometime. It's a beautiful wall across the street from the United Nations, and it's got the words of the prophet Isaiah on it: 'They shall beat their swords into plowshares and their spears into pruning hooks . . .'."

"What does that mean?"

"It means peace!" she said. "Weapons become tools for farming. That's a good idea, huh?" Diana laughed. "In America, of course, we'd call him the prophet Izzy!"

"Was he Jewish?" said Eli.

"Of course!"

"Why do you say of course?"

"Why? Because all of the prophets in the Bible are Jewish, honey."

"I didn't know that. How many are there?"

"I don't know," Diana said impatiently. "And you know what? It really doesn't matter how many, because it's what they *said* that counts. They were preaching for everybody, Eli. Peace is for everybody to make. Now, look: I told Avram that I'd be here. I left the house before him this morning, and maybe he forgot. If he calls, tell him where I am."

"Okay."

"I don't think they've yet voted inside the General Assembly," she went on in a nervous voice. "He's probably still in there, covering it."

"Okay."

"Are you sure you're all right?"

"Sure," Eli said. "Bye."

He hung up, thinking: "But it *does* matter. It does matter how many prophets, and who they were, and whether they're Jewish.

Why? I don't know. But it does! That's what Avram was saying. I mean, he's crazy to think we have to go to Israel, but . . . God, I wish she'd come home. Or at least call back." Eli wanted to remind Diana of that time when he'd seen her crying over the pictures of the burned Vietnamese kids—burned, in her eyes, to her mind, like Jewish kids in concentration camps. That's why she had cried—because she remembered, she knew, and so she *felt*.

"But Mom," Eli said out loud, "how am *I* going to feel those things?"

He paced into her bedroom, expecting to see signs of Avram's presence: a pair of shoes, some dirty clothes, a book. There was nothing, nothing out of order. "In fact," Eli thought, "where's his luggage and his typewriter?" He quickly checked every room in the house. Avram had left nothing—nothing except the feeling in Eli's stomach, the fear that the world was about to explode.

"I love your mother, you know that?" Suddenly that sounded to Eli like a way of saying goodbye.

Back in Diana's bedroom, he spotted her phone on the table by her bed and wished he could call her at the Isaiah Wall. Instead he called his father. "Dad?" he said, first thing. "Do you know what's going on at the United Nations?"

"No," said Allen, "what's going on at the United Nations?"

"Israel's getting into some kind of trouble."

"Ha! What else is new!"

"Dad?"

"Eli?"

"Do you think I could go there sometime?"

"Where, kiddo? To the U.N. or to Israel?"

Eli imagined Avram meeting him at the airport in Israel. "Elijah!" he would say. "Shalom Aleichem!"

"My name is Eli," Eli would reply. "Hello."

"Israel," he said to Allen. "Do you think I could go there sometime?"

"Are you serious?" Allen said.

"Yeah!" The butterflies in his stomach suddenly jumped into his chest.

"Well," said his father, "I don't see why not. I'm willing to talk with your mother about it. Have you?"

"No."

"Of course," Allen added, "we'd have to find a time when it's safe over there."

Commentary

The argument between Diana and Avram raises the much deeper question that faces every Jew: "What does it mean to be Jewish?" Diana seems to be saying that being Jewish means to believe in *tikun olam,* the healing of the world, and to engage in causes of social justice. Avram seems to be saying that the only way to be a full and loyal Jew is to make aliyah to Israel. Eli is like a ping-pong ball, batted back and forth between two positions.

In my opinion, both Diana and Avram are wrong. Though I have spent my whole life in Jewish social action, fighting for exactly those causes about which Diana is talking, I believe that being Jewish means more than doing good. Non-Jews are also interested in doing good. Martin Luther King, Jr., was not Jewish; nor was Mahatma Gandhi; nor is Nelson Mandela, the black hero of South Africa who has been in jail for twenty years for opposing racial injustice in his country. Social justice *is,* as Diana says, central to the Jewish religion. But it is not *all* there is to Judaism. If it were, a Jew could fulfill the obligations of a Jewish life by joining a political party, a peace group, or any civil liberties organization.

Social justice is at the *center* of Judaism, but the Jewish religion, which involves the relationship between the Jewish people and God, includes faith, prayer, holidays, education, historic memory, and religious practice. If, as Diana argues, Jews care deeply about "the stranger," it is because the Torah reminds us that we ourselves were once slaves and must, therefore, remember the heart of the stranger. This concept is reaffirmed at every Passover seder. But Diana and Eli do not belong to a synagogue, do not celebrate the Sabbath or Jewish holidays, and do not study their heritage. She talks about the prophets but knows very little about them. She cannot speak a word of Hebrew. Diana confuses being Jewish with being liberal. What about Jews who do not share her views on Vietnam or black rights or nuclear disarmament? Are they not true Jews? She's right about the Jewish passion for caring about the world, but she has plucked a lovely flower out of a splendid garden without a thought to tending the garden itself. If this garden of Judaism dies of neglect, the flower she waves will give off a brief fragrance and die. So might the Jewish people!

But her Israeli friend Avram isn't right either. He is dead wrong in comparing the Jewish community of America with that of Germany or Poland or anywhere else. America *is* different. That doesn't mean that something terrible could not happen to Jews here, but such an event is unlikely. The U.S. Constitution with its Bill of Rights, the good will of the American people, and the American tradition of fair play—all these protect us.

Moreover, if a catastrophe befell America's Jews, would Israel be safe? Israel depends on aid and support from America. Would that continue if America, God forbid, turned against us?

Furthermore, what makes Avram think that Israel is a safe place? Israel is surrounded by Arab nations pledged to its destruction, and it faces enormous internal problems as well. One serious problem is the deep conflict between ultra-Orthodox zealots, who control the religious life of Israel, and the majority of Israel's Jews, who are non-Orthodox (including Reform) Jews. The ultra-Orthodox do not recognize the legitimacy of Reform Judaism. A Reform (or Conservative or Reconstructionist) rabbi cannot officiate legally at a wedding or funeral in Israel. Some Orthodox leaders have even said that it is better for an Israeli to go to the beach on Yom Kippur than to pray in a Reform temple. All this raises the risk of a serious confrontation among Israeli Jews themselves.

Avram ignores the fact that even in Israel Jews can lose their Jewish identity. If ultra-Orthodoxy becomes the only option of religious life for Israelis, many will abandon religion. Without religious pluralism, Israeli Jews may live lives as far removed from the synagogue, Jewish holidays, and Jewish practices as Diana's life in America.

Israel is a proud center of Jewish life. Jews everywhere give its survival top priority. But it is foolish to believe that many American Jews, like Diana, are going to move to Israel. America is her home as Israel is Avram's. Visiting and loving Israel, learning Hebrew, and giving funds and political support are positive actions, but, in the end, American Jews have to build a strong Jewish life in America: stronger Jewish education for Jews of all ages; more dynamic synagogue life; Jewish homes that celebrate the Sabbath and the holidays; Jewish books and art in the home; and, as Diana says, concern for all human beings. I hope Eli listens to Diana and Avram, visits Israel and loves it, and then makes up his own mind.

Spraypaint Justice

Today, among the countries in the world, the United States has a minimum amount of anti-Semitism. Jewish Americans enjoy citizenship with the same privileges as other Americans. We can follow any career; we can live in any neighborhood; we can run for and get elected to any political office. We are entitled to what the United States Constitution calls "life, liberty, and the pursuit of happiness" the same as any other Americans.

But perhaps it would be better to say "almost" for each of these statements. We can follow *almost* any career—but if you look at the top-level jobs in many corporations, you'll find very few Jews. We can live in *almost* any neighborhood—but in certain neighborhoods, in some areas of the country, Jews are not welcome. We can run for *almost* any political office—yet no Jew has ever been nominated for president or vice-president of the U.S. by the Democrats or the Republicans.

Certainly it is true that there is very little ugly, violent anti-Semitism here. There are no anti-Jewish laws. There is no one telling us that we can't observe our religion, learn about our culture, or be Jewish in any way we please. But anti-Semitism does exist in America—in the hearts of some people.

In 1984, there were over 1,000 reported acts of anti-Semitism in the U.S. Most of these were acts of vandalism, like the painting of a swastika (the symbol of Nazism) on the door of a Jewish home or synagogue. There were also almost 400 threats or attacks against Jewish people and Jewish organizations, including three bombings and seventeen cases of arson (the crime of burning property). In addition, to be sure, there were hundreds of anti-Semitic insults and acts of discrimination that were *not* reported to the police or the Anti-Defamation League.

Why would incidents of anti-Semitism go unreported? Many Jews would rather ignore an insult than say anything about it, either because they're afraid to speak up or they're too busy to be bothered. We forget that, just twenty or thirty years ago, anti-Semitism was a much bigger problem in the U.S. than it is today. Jews were discriminated against in many ways. It took years of protest by Jews and non-Jews who cared about democracy before anti-Semitism began to decline in America. Therefore we should not forget the importance of speaking out. Unless we protest hatred and discrimination wherever and whenever it occurs, the problem will only get worse and will eventually affect all of us.

This is especially true for kids. *Almost all the anti-Semitic acts that are reported to the police or the Anti-Defamation League are committed by those under the age of twenty.* Many are teenagers who think what they're doing is funny. Only some are real Jew-haters. But all must be stopped. Anti-Semitism is never a laughing matter!

The question is: How do you stop them?

Cleveland, Ohio: 1986

Claudia stood with her back against the schoolyard fence, waiting for Ricky Carbone to show up. She kept telling herself, "I'm not going on a date with him. I'm just going to hang out with him for a while." That's exactly what Ricky had suggested, in fact: "C'mon, let's hang out after school. I'll buy you an ice cream if you let me watch you lick it!"

"Oh, God," Claudia thought, "he's got such a dirty mind! But so do all the boys. Anyway, this is definitely not a date—because if it was, my mom would kill me!" Claudia was not allowed to date alone. Going bowling or to the movies with a bunch of kids was fine, but dating alone? "Not until you're well along into high school," her mother often said.

Claudia could just imagine her mother saying it, now, with her chin raised high. "She's so snooty!" Claudia thought, and felt excited all over about Ricky's interest in her.

They had met a month before on opposite sides of a volleyball net, during the girls vs. boys varsity match in the gym. Claudia was the tallest girl on her team, and next year, when she jumped from the seventh to the ninth grades (she was in a Special Progress class), she would probably become the team captain. Ricky was the only guy on the boys' side who didn't hoot and tease all through the game. He just set his eye on Claudia every time he came up to serve and smashed the ball right at her.

While they were both playing at the net, he asked her name. Then he said in a low voice: "Boy, I'd rather be on your side—*at* your side, Claudia." And she had blushed and suddenly felt that her gym shorts were really too short and much too tight.

Claudia kept her eyes on the oak tree that overhung the fence and watched its leaves waving in the breeze. She didn't want to look like she was waiting for Ricky. She wanted him, instead, to come along and have a chance to admire her—her long, blonde hair, her denim skirt and black tights, her old sneakers. That way, if any of her friends happened to be around, they would think she had bumped into Ricky by accident.

"Maybe," Claudia worried, "I should have told him to meet me somewhere else?" That would have made it all seem too serious, too much like a date—but what if Sharon or Jennifer came along right after Rick and saw them together? It would be all over school by tomorrow morning, and Ricky would find out that Claudia was thirteen, not fourteen as she had told him. And everybody would start to ask her, "What's he like? What's he like?" And all of Ricky's friends would start asking the same question about her—only they wouldn't be talking about her personality! "Oh, God," Claudia moaned out loud, shaking her head.

Just at that moment, when she had given up her elegant pose

and had her hair in her eyes, she heard Ricky say, "Hey there, kid."

He had ridden up on his bicycle, a handsome, black ten-speed. "What did you do, cut all day?" Claudia asked, for she had expected to see him coming from the school building.

"Hell, no," he said. "I leave this baby right outside of school. Nobody in that place would be dumb enough to mess with my bike."

"Great," she said, "and what about the rest of the world?"

"Hey, no problem," he replied. "This is a nice, middle-class neighborhood, right? The only troublemakers in this neighborhood are the ones I hang around with! C'mon." He patted the bar in front of his bicycle seat. "Let's go for a soda or something."

"Oh, no," Claudia said. "I'm not getting on that bike unless you let *me* on the seat and *you* take the bumps."

"Hey, didn't anybody ever tell you that boys have different equipment? I'd ruin myself on there." Ricky swung his leg over the seat like a cowboy and began to walk alongside of her, guiding his bicycle with one hand.

They went first for ice cream, then to a record store because, Ricky said, he "felt like spending some money." It was strange for Claudia to be alone with him this way; for a month she'd seen him only among crowds of kids in school, and only for brief moments. As they talked, now, Claudia began to realize that their relationship was really just a big flirtation. She had thought he was cute; he had thought she was foxy. She had giggled at all his jokes; he had joked to make her giggle. Oh, yes, he was different from her friends, including all the boys she had ever liked, and that was pretty exciting. He was older, and he was not Jewish ("My mother," Claudia thought, "would murder me!"), and he was tough and sassy and good-looking like Clint Eastwood. But when it came right down to it, his "different" qualities were really pretty boring. "Different," she thought—"like he never reads a book! Different—he likes junk movies. Different—he never says what he's thinking, just tells stories to impress me."

Inside the record store, he pulled her by the arm to the heavy metal section. "Oh, God," Claudia thought, "this is awful. Am I stuck-up, or what?" Even Ricky's good looks were beginning to seem a little wooden, a little empty, like a mannequin.

"I'm really not into heavy metal," Claudia said.

"Yeah? What are you into?"

Claudia shrugged. ("Why am I shrugging?" she asked herself. "I know what I like!") "Jazz," she said. "My mom's big on jazz, so I've gotten to know it some. And all kinds of rock—except heavy metal. The heavy metal bands can't play, so they make you deaf, instead. You ought to listen," she suggested, "to some rhythm and blues. That's the best."

"Like what groups?" Ricky said.

"Old stuff, you know—James Brown, B.B. King, Aretha . . ."

Ricky snorted and nodded. "Nigger music."

"Excuse me?"

"Hard-core nigger music," he said. "You really like that stuff? I mean, you're not talking about Michael Jackson, right? He's nothing but a white faggot in a nigger's body anyway."

"Uch!" Claudia cried. "You're disgusting!" But she had said that to him a dozen times since they'd met, whenever he teased her about being sexy. So Ricky just smiled, thinking he was fresh. He went over to the cashier to pay for a Twisted Sister cassette. Claudia stayed by the record rack, wondering how to get away from him.

"C'mon," he called, standing over by the door. She didn't like the tone of his voice. It made her feel like he owned her. She thought about starting an argument with him then and there, but she knew what really was upsetting her: those words he'd used, disgusting words with loud echoes. But it was too late now. Why hadn't she said something at the very moment he used them? "Oh, God, I'm sorry," she thought, looking at a poster of Michael Jackson that was hanging over the doorway as she followed Ricky out of the store.

He was putting the cassette into the saddlebag behind his bicycle seat. Claudia spotted a can of something in there. "What's that?" she said, pointing.

"Nasty drugs," he said with a leer, "that make your clothes fall off."

Claudia rolled her eyes. "Really, what is it?"

"Nothing. A can of spraypaint. I'm doing a project."

"Really?" Could there be something actually interesting about the guy? "What kind of project? Do you build stuff?"

"Hell, no," he said. "I buy whatever I need. Listen, how about coming to the park?"

Claudia stepped back and shook her head. Her words bubbled out like soda from a can that's been shaken. "I can't, I've got to be home, I've got something to do for my mom. You know, when I mentioned her inside the store, I remembered, I had promised her . . ."

Ricky shrugged. "Suit yourself. Hey, what's your last name?"

"Why?"

"C'mon, what is it?"

"Rothman."

He nodded. "Uh-huh." Then he winked at her. "Take a walk in the park tomorrow, and you'll see your name on every rock."

"Oh, God! Ricky, don't you dare!"

"Hey, enjoy your jazz, all right?" Then he swung onto his bicycle and left her standing there.

In the evening, Jennifer called. "So how did it go?"

"With what?" Claudia said.

"With Ricky Carbone! C'mon, Claudi, you can't do anything without my knowing it?"

"I don't believe it!" Claudia squealed. "How did you find out?"

"Ricky's friends have big mouths," Jennifer said. "So c'mon! How did it go?"

"It didn't," Claudia said miserably. "He creeped me out."

"Why, what happened?"

"I don't know . . . Jenny? You think it's all right for us to go with boys who aren't Jewish?"

"Sure, what's the difference? I mean, as long as they're not animals, you know? Like Jeffrey Shapiro, Mr. Basketball? You wouldn't go out with him either, right? And he wears a Magen David around his neck."

"I don't know," Claudia said. "The Italian kids seem to, like, get older quicker."

"What did he do, try to feel you up?"

"Jennifer!"

"What? C'mon, Claudi, he's a ninth-grader, whether he's Jewish or not. Ricky Carbone's had hair on his chest for years!"

"Oh, God!" Claudia moaned in embarrassment.

"If you'd told me in advance," Jennifer scolded her, "I could have warned you."

"Warned me about what?" Claudia said. "That he's a dummy? That he talks like a . . . like a . . ." She sighed. "Anyway, I didn't even spend two hours with him, all right? He grossed me out. Only now I'm afraid to show my face tomorrow. He had a can of spraypaint. He said he was going to write my name all over the park."

"Forget it," Jennifer said. "He probably doesn't even know how to spell it." They both laughed and moved on to other subjects.

But later that night, Ricky himself phoned. Claudia's mother answered it and called upstairs to her daughter. "How'd you get my number?" was Claudia's first question.

"On the bathroom wall at McDonald's."

This time she treated him to silence.

"It's in the phone book," he said.

"How'd you know my mother's name?"

"I didn't."

"Well, there are at least five or six Rothman's in South Euclid."

"Six," he said. "And you're the fourth one I'm trying. So what's happening?"

"Nothing," she said coldly.

"Did you help your mommy like a good little girl?"

She wanted to curse him and hang up, but she feared his revenge: that can of spraypaint. Again she was silent.

"Where's your father?" Ricky said. "You got a father?"

"Of course I have a father—though I doubt if you have a mother! My parents are divorced."

"Aw, poor baby."

Claudia heard a clicking in the phone. "Where are you calling from?" she said.

"A pizza place. Listen, if you two ladies are all alone, maybe I ought to come on over. . . ."

"Cut it out, Ricky, okay?"

"Your mom as good-looking as you?"

"Why? Is your mom as sick in the head as you?"

"Aw, you love it," he said.

"Yeah, I love it," she repeated with disgust.

"You know, Claudia," he said, his voice rising, "you had me fooled with that long blonde hair of yours."

"What do you mean, 'fooled'?" she said. "It's my real color."

"Yeah? And Rothman's your real name?"

"What's that supposed to mean?" But Claudia knew perfectly well what it meant. At every family gathering, her relatives would always comment on her blonde hair. Her older aunts and uncles, especially, said she looked like "a real Hollywood *shiksa,*" a gentile glamour girl.

Ricky was putting her down for being Jewish.

"So listen," he said, "if I can't come over, how about you coming out?"

Claudia was trembling, half in fear and half in anger. "Why don't *you* go spray paint in your ear," she said, "and fill up the white space in there?"

"Whoa! Drop dead, OK?" Then—damn it!—he hung up first.

"Who was that, honey?" her mother asked as Claudia came downstairs.

"Just a jerk from school."

"Oh, and what makes him a jerk?"

"I don't know," Claudia said irritably as she trudged into the living room to watch television. "Maybe it's in his blood. He eats so much pasta that now he's got spaghetti for a brain."

"He's an Italian boy?"

"And how!"

"Let's not be prejudiced," her mother warned.

"Sorry," Claudia said. "But he really does have a Neanderthal mind."

What was that light flashing outside her window? And that noise, like static from a radio? Claudia glanced at the clock by the side of her bed. It was 1:45 in the morning. "What's going on?" She threw aside her blanket and stepped to the window.

A police car was parked down the block, in front of the Beth Israel Temple. The flasher on top of the car was bouncing red and white beams of light off the surrounding buildings. Claudia threw open her window and ducked her head out to see better. Now she could clearly hear the police car radio, that crackling sound that had woken her. Many of her neighbors were milling around out there, some dressed, some in bathrobes. But even with the cop car light, Claudia couldn't see what was going on.

Suddenly the lawn lights of the synagogue came on and flooded the building. "My God!" Claudia gasped.

There was a huge swastika spraypainted on the synagogue doors.

She pulled her head back inside as if someone had thrown a rock at her. Her first thought was: "I don't believe this. This is like a movie, a weird movie." Ricky Carbone had spraypainted that thing—she would have bet money on that fact. He had done it because she had rejected him and acted stuck-up. "Oh, my God, and if I tell," Claudia thought, sitting on the edge of her bed, "the whole neighborhood's going to know who I've been going out with." She could just see herself, pleading with her mom: "We didn't even go out! It wasn't even a date!"

"Yeah, but you flirted with him, didn't you?" Claudia scolded herself. "You made him think he was hot stuff, didn't you? You thought you were so sexy and grown up. Airhead!"

She dragged herself back to the window, hoping, like a little girl, that if she looked again . . . but there it was, in bright red. Some of the neighbors were already trying to scrub the swastika from the doors. Claudia wanted to help, to make up for the trouble she had caused, but she was afraid that they'd suspect her for being so eager, for being awake, for working to clean the synagogue when she hardly ever used the synagogue. And then they would start to ask questions. . . .

"That stupid creep!" Claudia thought. "Why did he have to do it on the synagogue? Why couldn't he do it on my door? 'Claudia is a dirty Jew,' or 'Claudia is a lousy JAP'? I mean, I don't care *what* he thinks, but now it's like *everybody*'s involved! God!" She threw herself on the bed and rolled from side to side as if she had a fever.

The red paint of the swastika was gone by morning, but its shape was still there, like a bleach stain. A police car was parked in front, and a couple of television reporters were talking with people as they passed the synagogue. Claudia avoided them by circling around the block on her way to school. She kept thinking: "Maybe I should go back. I could look right into the TV camera and say, 'Ricky Carbone, you're the most disgusting person I know.' But then the police would get involved; and I'd have to testify; and Ricky would get to drag my name and my reputation in the dirt. No, no," Claudia told herself, "I don't need to have my love life advertised all over Cleveland. This is between Ricky Carbone and Claudia Rothman. Period!"

It seemed she was right, too, for nobody in school was talking about the vandalism, while she couldn't get it off her mind. Claudia kept listening to conversations in the hall between classes, wondering if anybody knew. Finally in the lunchroom she got to ask Jennifer. "Jenny, did you hear what happened to the synagogue on my block?"

Jennifer nodded and bit her sandwich. "Sure. They make such a big deal out of graffiti, you know?"

"But it was a swastika!"

Jennifer shrugged. "So somebody's got a weird sense of humor."

Claudia clucked her tongue. "It's worse than that," she said, then stopped herself from arguing. She knew there was nothing funny about painting a swastika on a synagogue or any place. It was a *lot* worse than graffiti on walls or statues or subway cars— a *lot* worse because the swastika meant death to the Jews. The swastika meant the Holocaust. The swastika was something from a nightmare. But Jenny was too smart and too curious, and Claudia knew that an argument would only lead to the question, "Why, do you know who did it?" Instead she kept her mouth shut. For a moment she felt ashamed and frustrated, as she had felt in the record store when Ricky had started talking about "niggers" and she had said nothing. Then she pushed away the feeling with anger, thinking: "What a bigoted creep he is! It *had* to be him, I'm sure! Didn't he say that his friends are the only troublemakers in the neighborhood? And I *saw* that can of spraypaint right there in his saddlebag. God! I wish I could beat him up myself. . . ."

Suddenly Claudia heard a voice in the lunchroom—a voice that spoke her thoughts, answered her prayers. "I'm going to do something about it, too, if I can find out who it is. Jews have got to protect themselves, that's all. I'll kick his butt from here to Germany!"

"Uch," Jennifer said, "he's such an animal."

The "animal" was Jeffrey Shapiro, the tallest boy in the lunch-room. He was talking to his friends about the vandalism in a loud, bragging voice, as if to challenge whoever had done it to a good, bloody fistfight. Claudia looked around to see if Ricky Carbone was anywhere in the lunchroom. Jennifer, thinking her friend was looking for Jeffrey, jerked her thumb over her shoulder. "He's right behind you."

Claudia nodded. Ricky Carbone was *not* around, or else, Claudia was sure, he would have come by to taunt her. She grabbed her notebook and began to write furiously. "Hey, what are you doing?" Jennifer asked. "Wait! Where are you going?" Claudia had torn the page from her notebook and was folding it as she stood up.

"Sh," she said to Jennifer. "I'm going to bring two animals into the same cage and see what happens."

"Claudi!" Jennifer cried, calling everyone's attention to Claudia as she walked over to Jeffrey Shapiro's table.

"Claudi!" two of Shapiro's friends yelled in high, silly voices. Another of the boys made chirping sounds.

Claudia stopped at the table and looked Jeffrey Shapiro in the eye. "Do you know how to read?" she said.

"Get lost, Rothman," Jeffrey replied.

"Why don't you answer me?" she said. "I know you're great with a basketball. How about with this?" She held out the folded note. A boy pinched her rear end. She elbowed him hard, and everyone at the table laughed. "Can you read it to yourself," she asked Shapiro, "or does this whole gang of jerks have to read it to you?"

Shapiro stood—all six feet of him—and took the note. "Thanks. I didn't know you cared."

"What's it say? What's up?" the boy who had pinched Claudia wanted to know.

"Bug off," Jeffrey said to him and walked away from the table to read Claudia's note in privacy.

"What in the world was that all about?" Jennifer asked as Claudia returned to her seat. "Claudi! Tell me!"

She was watching Shapiro. He finished reading her note and folded it into his pocket, then looked at her and nodded.

Claudia smiled and lowered her eyes. "There," she said to Jennifer in a low voice. "I just ruined Ricky Carbone's day, for real."

Her heart was beating like a bass drum as she left the school at the end of the day. She walked so slowly that Jennifer kept nagging her. "C'mon! What are you, some kind of turtle?"

They were passing the schoolyard. There was a crowd of kids swelling in there, watching something. They were all very quiet. "This is it," thought Claudia, and her blood ran hot.

She stopped and watched through the fence. The crowd opened up to make way for someone. It was Ricky Carbone, running, with a bloody nose and torn shirt. Jeffrey Shapiro was after him. Claudia froze in her tracks.

Shapiro lunged, caught him around the waist, and pulled him to the ground. They rolled, punching each other and cursing. Claudia could hear the thuds of their fists. It was nothing like in the movies.

Shapiro crawled on top of Ricky. "All right, man, all right, man!" Ricky wailed. "I give! I give! All right? What the hell are you doing? Get off!"

Jeffrey punched him in the face again. Ricky's head bounced against the pavement. "My God," Claudia murmured, "that's enough already."

"Uch," Jennifer groaned, "they're such pigs. C'mon, let's go."

"He deserves it," Claudia said.

"You want to watch this stuff?"

Claudia nodded slowly.

"Why? One date and you hate Ricky that much?"

"He's the one who spraypainted the synagogue," Claudia said. "That's what I told Jeffrey today in the lunchroom."

"You're kidding!" Jennifer cried. "And how do you know?"

The fight was spreading. Friends of Ricky's had begun to pull Jeffrey off him, which brought Jeffrey's friends out of the crowd with their fists flying.

"He called me last night," Claudia said, "and he said stuff to me—anti-Semitic stuff. I told him to go spraypaint between his ears. Then just a few hours later the synagogue was vandalized."

"So what does that prove?" Jennifer shouted. "And I can't believe that Jeffrey just believed you! Look at them! My God, Claudia, Ricky doesn't even know where you live!"

"Oh, come on, Jennifer! He got my number out of the phone book. He could just as easily—no, wait . . ." Claudia had just remembered: her mother didn't list their address in the phone book.

"Just this morning," Jennifer insisted, "Ricky was bothering me to tell him where you live! He said he wanted to send flowers."

"That's an act," Claudia said coldly. "That's crazy. It's an act, Jennifer. Don't believe him. He did that swastika!"

"Well, if it's so important to you," Jennifer replied, "then why didn't you tell the police, or the rabbi, or the school administration—someone?" She waved her hand towards the playground. "You think *this* is better? What's it going to prove?"

Claudia stubbornly repeated what she'd heard Jeffrey Shapiro say in the lunchroom, "Jews have got to protect themselves!"

"Oh, you're just saying that, Claudia. You know that's bull! You're not protecting anything, you're just getting back at Ricky."

"I am not!" Claudia shouted. "He did it and he deserves whatever he gets!"

"Great!" said Jennifer. "And next time you do something I don't like, I'll just get a gun and shoot you!"

"Oh, come on, Jennifer! I'm telling you, he . . . Look, I'll prove it!" She pointed through the fence. "That's Ricky's bicycle. I'll bet you any amount that there's a can of red spraypaint in the saddlebag."

Claudia ran to the gate and into the yard. The fight was over. Ricky was lying on the ground, crying. Claudia snuck over to his bicycle, parked against the fence. She reached into the saddlebag and felt the can. "Here it is!" she called to Jennifer and held it up to the fence.

But the can had a green cap. "Wait a minute." Claudia popped it off and sprayed. Green paint. "Oh, my God."

Commentary

"Spraypaint Justice" is a fascinating story with a surprise ending that has the impact of a kick in the stomach. But let's back up for a moment and look at the story in detail.

It's clearly about bigotry. But just who are the bigots, and how do they reveal their prejudices?

Ricky is the apparent villain of this piece, and Claudia concludes that he is not only a jerk but an anti-Semite as well. Is she right? What is the evidence in the story? Ricky is clearly anti-black as you can see from his ugly racist statements about Michael Jackson and black music. But if he's anti-black, does it follow that he's also anti-Jewish? My own answer to that is no. As a matter of fact, there are some Jews who are anti-black and some blacks who are anti-Jewish. But, on the whole, studies and experience show that Nazis, KKK members, and other bigots *do* tend to hate blacks and Jews in common. People who have an inner need to hate do not usually limit their poison to one group. It spreads like cancer, poisoning the whole system.

So is Ricky an anti-Semite? If you were a lawyer, what proof could you find in the story? Hardly any. We know that Ricky may not have spraypainted the swastika on the synagogue. What *did* he do and say that makes him an anti-Semite? He did tell Claudia that she had almost "fooled" him with that real blond hair—meaning, of course, that she didn't *look* Jewish. Stupid and narrow yes—but anti-Semitic? More likely, Ricky had a fixed picture in his head—a stereotype—of what Jews look like, of how Jews act, of how they think, and what they believe. Obviously, Claudia did not fit his stereotype. Does that make him anti-Jewish?

What complicates matters in the story is that Claudia also has stereotypes about other groups—in this case, Italians. Exactly what is her stereotype of Italians? Remember, she exclaims to her mother that this guy is a jerk and "Maybe it's in his blood. He eats so much pasta that now he's got spaghetti for a brain." To which Claudia's mother murmurs, "Now let's not be prejudiced." Well, is her mother right? Is Claudia prejudiced against Italians? When Claudia sees how dumb and shallow Ricky really is, does she explain to herself that it's because Ricky is Italian, not Jewish, or just because he happens to be dumb and shallow?

Let's take it one step further. In the telephone conversation between Claudia and her friend, Jennifer, Claudia raises the question, "Is it all right for us to go with boys who aren't Jewish?" What's your own answer to that question? Whatever your answer, do you think it is prejudiced to *ask* that question? Do you agree with Jennifer's answer?

There are several interesting issues in this story. One is the terrible hurt of bigotry; another is the sin of being silent in the face of bigotry. To be silent when somebody is spouting hate is to be an accomplice. In our story, Ricky was guilty of an ugly outburst in the record shop. Claudia mildly disapproved, but she didn't really take a stand. How should she have handled it? What could she have said to Ricky? Perhaps Claudia overreacted and lashed out at Ricky *later* because she was so angry at *herself* for not standing up to him in the record shop.

Violence is obviously not the correct answer to prejudice. What good did it do to unleash that bully and unguided missile, Shapiro? He said, "Jews must protect themselves," and that's okay—but how? By beating up innocent persons? In fact, the Jewish organization called the Jewish Defense League (JDL) shares the same macho point of view. It actually operates camps in America to train young Jews in karate and marksmanship. What's your reaction to this? If not by physical self-defense, then how should we react to anti-Semites?

The deepest moral of this story is one of fair play. In American democracy, a person is innocent until proven guilty. Ricky is not a very admirable boy, but Claudia convicted him for a crime he may or may not have committed. Not only did Claudia convict him, but she also had the chutzpah to sentence him to a beating from a Jewish bully who never bothered to check out Claudia's charge.

What should Claudia have done when she learned the synagogue was vandalized? To whom should she have spoken? Why didn't she do that? What Claudia did was act like judge, jury, and executioner. She was using "guilt by association"—Ricky had a spraycan, the synagogue was sprayed, therefore Ricky did it. Even in America, many innocent persons have suffered loss of careers and reputations as a result of public campaigns based on "guilt by association." Jews especially must defend the Constitutional guarantee of "due process" in law to insure that justice and not prejudice prevails in America.

So this story contains many important truths:

• Don't let bigotry go unanswered—speak up.
• Judge each person as an individual—not as an Italian, a Jew, a black, or member of any group.

- Violence only begets violence; it solves nothing.
- Fair play is vital, even in dealing with foul play.

The old proverb, "Fight fire with fire," usually results in burning down the house. Fighting fire with water is much more sensible. Ricky may be a nasty kid, but he is entitled to due process and fair play. That's the democratic way; it's also the Jewish way.

Whether or not Ricky was the one who did the deed, the temple was subjected to an anti-Semitic assault. For members of the temple who were old enough to have lived through the hell of the Nazi era, the painting of a swastika on the door must have stirred up terrible fears. Anti-Jewish vandalism of this kind—daubing synagogues, defacing Jewish cemeteries, spraypainting Jewish homes—has been increasing in America in recent years.

Does that mean that anti-Semitism is on the rise? Maybe yes, maybe no. It could mean simply that the police are doing a better job of keeping records of such incidents. It could also mean that many juveniles are using this kind of vandalism to blow off steam and to do mischief. While the guilty should be punished, their deeds should not be viewed as a major danger.

Sometimes the culprit turns out to be a Jew! Not long ago in Hartford, Connecticut, there was a bad rash of anti-Jewish vandalism, including swastika-daubings and even anti-Jewish death threats. Naturally, the Jewish community got scared and angry. Rewards were offered to help catch the offender. Hartford seemed to be in the midst of a campaign of anti-Semitic terror. In the end, the culprit turned out to be a mentally-disturbed Jewish teenager. This shows—as our spraypaint story does—how important it is to keep cool, not rush to conclusions, and not resort to guilt by association.

In almost every case where anti-Jewish attacks take place, the entire community rises up to express its outrage. The police do all in their power to track down the guilty persons. Judges crack down hard on the vandals. When the synagogue needs to be repainted or renovated, Christian church groups often come forward to help with the work. If the synagogue is damaged, a neighboring church usually invites the Jewish community to use its

facilities while the damage is repaired. The newspapers and television express the conscience of the community in condemning
bigotry and vandalism. So when desecrations occur, Jews find
support from the non-Jewish community and do not feel alone or
abandoned as Jews did for many centuries in Europe.

Besides, there is another piece of evidence—even more important. Even though the number of incidents has increased, it does
not follow that anti-Semitism is increasing. Subways and buses,
churches of all kinds, public and private schools, and other public
buildings are being subjected to defacement, window-smashing,
graffiti, and daubings. This epidemic of petty violence seems to
provide an outlet for certain sick minds, often belonging to
youngsters. It stinks—but is it anti-Semitism, even if it includes
swastikas and other such symbols?

Actually, while anti-Jewish vandalism has increased, other studies of anti-Semitism show an opposite trend. These show that
anti-Jewish attitudes in America are actually declining. In other
words, the percentage of the population that holds anti-Semitic
stereotypes—"the Jews control TV" "Jews are rich," "Jews are
Communists"—is getting smaller, not larger. A larger and larger
percentage of non-Jews would not object to having a Jewish
neighbor next door or being represented by a Jewish legislator
or having a Jewish business partner or marrying a Jew. And, in
any case, the laws are now so tough that even an anti-Semite
cannot prevent a Jew from moving next door or renting an apartment in his building or running for office or exercising his full
civil rights in every way.

I don't care whether an individual likes Jews or hates them.
What I *do* care about is that a prejudiced person cannot *act* by
discriminating against me as a Jew. In other words, I don't care
if a restaurant owner has nutty ideas about Jews as long as the
restaurant is open to all people, regardless of race or religion,
and gives me the same good service that all other customers get.

Wait a minute; I take that back! If the owner has made known
those anti-Semitic feelings, I would take my business elsewhere.
Why reward a bigot?

Some American cities have faced anti-Semitic incidents that are much more severe than vandalism. One was Skokie, Illinois, a town in which more than half the population is Jewish, including many survivors of the Nazi Holocaust. The American Nazi Party applied for a license to march in full uniform through the streets of Skokie. The town was deeply torn. On one hand, even hate groups have freedom of speech and freedom of assembly; on the other hand, Jews who had survived Hitler's Holocaust also have rights. The Jewish community went to court to try to prevent the march. In the end, the courts declared that even Nazis had the right to march; but they ordered the march to take place in Chicago instead of the more explosive atmosphere of Skokie, where violence could have resulted. Some Jews saw the Skokie/Nazi episode as proof of the strength of anti-Semitism in America. Others pointed out that all segments of America were on the side of the Jews and that a handful of clowns, even dressed up as Nazis, does not represent a real danger. If you had lived in Skokie—or if a similar group wants to demonstrate in your town—what position would you take? If the Jewish Defense League threatened to beat up the Nazis and break up their parade, what would you say or do? How would you feel about a counter-demonstration of the decent citizens of town—the mayor, clergymen, editors, civic leaders, etc.—to show that the hatemongers represent nothing but their own rotten prejudices?